"An engaging debut... Kristoph skillfully connects three independent perspectives to demonstrate how an individual choice, whether self-serving or for the greater good, can create a ripple of consequences in unexpected ways."

-PUBLISHERS WEEKLY

"Concise and picturesque... this book is a gem."

-MANHATTAN BOOK REVIEW

"Moving stories that feature plenty of conflict and drama."

-SAN FRANCISCO BOOK REVIEW

"Kristoph does an excellent job of drawing the reader into the story. The character development is fantastic... the clearly descriptive apocalyptic setting permeates each page."

-READERVIEWS

BOOKS BY
DAVID KRISTOPH

Tales of a Dying Star

Siege of Praetar

The Ancillary

Sword of Blue

Drowned by Fire

Born of Sand

Ultimate Ending Books

Treasures of the Forgotten City

The House on Hollow Hill

The Ship at the Edge of Time

Enigma at the Greensboro Zoo

The Secret of the Aurora Hotel

The Strange Physics of the Heidelberg Laboratory

The Tower of Never There

Sabotage in the Sundered Sky

Tales of a Dying Star

Book I: Siege of Praetar

Cover design by Milan Jaram

Editing by Briana Kirby

Enjoyed this book? Please take the time to leave a review
on Amazon.

To my grandfather Robert, for explaining the universe.

Tales of a Dying Star

Part I: The Sentinel

Tales of a Dying Star

Chapter 1

Alarms flashed red in the cockpit. Hyken woke with a jerk.

A button clicked beneath his finger and the noise stopped, leaving only the blinking red light. *I was daydreaming*, he thought, not willing to admit to himself he slept in earnest. He'd been back on Melis with his children, playing in the meadow where the river bent and foamed.

He touched a button and a ship appeared on the glass monitor. Another tap and its details were listed: Ouranos-class freighter, scanned at three thousand and six tonnes, leaving the planet's atmosphere and beginning its turn. They were common here in the inner system, used for hauling goods or refined metals ready for industrial use. He could see it with his naked eye now, a tiny speck of light moving away from Praetar, the hazy yellow planet that filled most of the cockpit window.

That's not right, Hyken thought, recalling the facts and figures he'd memorized long ago. A quick glance at another screen confirmed it: the ship was underweight for its class by seventy tonnes. His fingers tapped at the screen and his view improved, zooming-in on the fast-moving craft. It was unremarkable, no paint or markings to set it apart from any other ship. He didn't detect any concealed weapons, but the humans on Praetar were crafty in their engineering, and he knew the freighter was malicious. It certainly wasn't hauling goods. He supposed it didn't matter; his orders were clear regardless of the threat.

He pushed two buttons and flicked a switch. His ship shuddered from the launch. Two small missiles streaked away, visible in the window of the cockpit as they arced toward the freighter. It was over within seconds, the missiles finding their destination and puffing into a silent explosion in the distance. When the flames faded nothing remained but a thin cloud of smoke marring his view of the planet. The blinking light ceased, returning the cockpit to its former peace.

They never saw Hyken's ship, a Sentinel-class fighter that was coated black and invisible to detection. He liked that just fine. The disc-shaped Sentinels were small and slow, good for striking first from the shadows but unable to flee or fight any legitimate threat. It had no other defenses. A freighter retrofitted with weapons of its own would have made quick work of him if the missiles had missed. Hyken tried not to think about that.

"What was that?" asked his copilot Alard, appearing in the doorway to the cockpit. He scratched the back of his neck and squinted at the screens. "The launch woke me."

He was a young scruff, on his first tour and still barely a man. *No family of his own yet, poor kid.* He was competent at his post though, at least in the three days they'd been together. "Freighter up from Praetar. Moving fast, underweight. Probably hidden weapon systems on board."

Alard leaned over and read the instruments. "Did you run a deeper scan?"

"Nope. We've our orders, no need to waste the energy. Unless you think otherwise." Hyken let a bit of authority trickle into his voice.

Alard shrugged and sat in the second chair. "Did I miss anything else?"

"Nope, it's been quiet," Hyken replied. "You can go back to sleep; you've got another hour."

"I'm awake now." Alard pulled a small pouch from his uniform pocket, adjusting a nozzle at one end. He squeezed the bag into his mouth and the smell of coffee filled the room.

Hyken watched him out of the corner of his eye, but said nothing. It was always tough to gauge a rookie, and Alard was quieter than most. They sat there for a long while before Hyken could no longer bear the silence.

"Don't tell the siege commander," he said, leaning over to confide in the other crewmember, "but I was daydreaming before the freighter appeared."

Alard probably didn't care, but was polite enough to feign interest. "Oh? What about?"

"I was back on Melis with my boys. They're eight and three. Jon's the eldest. He has my eyes, but Cairne's got my personality. We were playing in a field near our home, throwing rocks in the river. The boys started throwing the rocks as far as they could, arguing over who had the stronger arm."

Alard listened politely, "Mmm hmm."

"I had Cairne composed after my fourth tour, mind you. It was all legitimate; none of that business on the black market. As if the peacekeepers wouldn't find out."

His co-pilot said nothing, and it occurred to Hyken that maybe he was being rude. *Here I am blabbering about my biological riches when this one has none of his own.* So he said, "How many children do you want?"

His co-pilot shrugged. "I don't know. It's only my first tour."

"I know, I know. I mean when all is done and finished, beyond your second. Surely you have an idea of how many you want."

Alard took another long pull from his coffee and stared out the window before answering. "I may not do a second. Right now I just want to complete my time and become a civilian again."

Hyken frowned, confused. "Is it the second tour you're afraid of? Or do you not want children at all?"

"Either. Both. I don't know, I've no heart for this work." He realized what he'd said, and quickly added, "I'm happy to serve the Emperor, don't get me wrong. But I would be content to return home for good after this. And children..." He furrowed his brow at the glass and said, "They're a lot of work, a burden even. And I haven't any women in mind."

"You don't need 'em," Hyken said cheerfully. "I've no wife, but I have my boys. The technicians just need a bit of your DNA, and you can pick the rest out from a database."

He shrugged again. "Yeah, sure. I've just never felt that pull, that desire, you know?"

Hyken *didn't* know. What was it all for, if not to reproduce, to bring life into existence? It saddened him to hear Alard dismiss it so easily. *The boy's too young, he doesn't know what he wants just yet.* That would change in time, as he matured and earned a greater appreciation for life.

"We all have an obligation to create life," he said.

"There are plenty of people to do that," Alard pointed out. "Planets full of them."

"Sure, but that's their *job.* Their intention isn't pure. Life is something to be cherished and savored, not created in a factory."

Alard only shrugged.

13

"What about your family?" Hyken asked. "The one you grew up with."

"What about them?"

"Do you have any siblings? Or a mother?"

"I have three sisters. I'm the only boy."

Hyken gaped at him. "Four children? Your father completed eight tours, then?"

Alard nodded. "He's on his tenth. He's... a high-ranking officer, in the Exodus Fleet."

Hyken whistled through his teeth and looked at the kid with new respect. He'd never heard of anyone completing ten tours, or at least surviving that long. Hyken's own five tours seemed meager by comparison.

"You must be proud to be his son, to share such a man's blood."

"Sure," he said, but there was no heart in his voice. Hyken arched an eyebrow at him, and Alard explained, "He's a hero and all that. He was with the first force to capture Praetar thirty years ago," he said, nodding out the window. "But I don't know him very well beyond that."

"You don't know him?" Hyken's mouth twisted. "He's your *father.*"

"I've only met him a handful of times. I've spent more time with you in this Sentinel in the past three days than in a lifetime with him." Alard cocked his head at the pilot. "How often do you see your children?"

"Once every two years, in between tours," he said. He

didn't like the accusation in Alard's voice, so he jabbed a finger at him and said, "And you can believe they know their father."

There was plenty of information on Hyken's career in the computers for his boys to learn; he'd instructed their custodian to make them study every week. He sent them letters on their born-day, besides, which was more than most children could hope for. *I'm lucky to have such loyal boys*, he thought, scowling at his co-pilot. What kind of a son didn't care enough to learn about his blood?

Alard put up his hands. "I'm sorry, I didn't mean to insult. Are you happy with two? How many tours will you do?"

"As many as I can," Hyken said cheerfully. "I was born for this sort of work. There's no greater calling, no fuller pride, than defending the Empire." When Alard said nothing, Hyken added, "You are proud to defend the empire, at least?"

"Sure," Alard said, studying the information on one of the glass screens intently.

Hyken was unconvinced of his piety, but didn't ask more. Instead, he said, "I'd compose enough children to fill a planet, if they let me. So I'll do enough tours to make as many as I can, and be content with that."

"Aren't you scared? Afraid to die after so many tours?"

Hyken laughed in earnest. "Stars, no. And I'll tell you

15

why not." He leaned close to Alard, as if to confide in him. "We're all going to die, here or at home or in some faraway system. Our bodies will be burned away to ash, like so many flecks of light across the stars. But my eyes will live on through Jon, and my curled hair with Cairne, and my freckled skin with the both of them. Through my children, and their children, and their children's children, I will live forever. Reproduction gives us a chance at immortality."

He held Alard's gaze a moment longer to let the words sink in. The co-pilot leaned back in his chair and stared off into nothing, considering. Finally he said, "That's nice."

Hyken smiled, satisfied. "It's the truth."

The ship's alarm screamed at them, bathing the cockpit in red light once again. They both whirled to their instruments, clicking buttons and swiping at the glass monitors. A ship jumped into view on the screen, another Ouranos-class freighter. Hyken looked up from his screen and gazed out the window, squinting in the distance until he saw it, a small point of light drifting away from the yellow planet.

"Seventy tonnes underweight, like the other," Hyken said. The other man nodded. "I couldn't detect any hidden weapon systems on the last one, but believe me they're there. Don't trust the Praetari for a second or it will bite you in the ass. You want to do the honors?"

Alard frowned at the instruments. "The missile bays are empty."

"Shit," Hyken muttered, swiveling his chair to another terminal. The Sentinel remained concealed by using as little power as possible; tasks that were automatic on most ships had to be initiated manually, when their safety was certain. That included reloading the missiles, which he'd forgotten to do. *I would have done it immediately, if that boy hadn't come up here asking about my family.* His fingers danced across the instruments.

"Ship's turning toward us," Alard said, alarm creeping into his voice. "We'll be in range of standard beams in forty-five seconds, if they're armed like you think."

Hyken glanced back to the screen and saw that he was right. "It's just a coincidence that they're flying this way. They've no way to detect our ship."

"Unless they have a Kalari scanner," Alard said, "then they'd see us just fine. Forty seconds."

"First missile's done, second one loading." He stared at the computer's blinking light, and muttered a silent prayer to the Emperor.

Alard tapped his foot nervously. "Should I cut on the engine, in case we need to move?"

"It won't be ready in time. And I wouldn't want to reveal the Sentinel, even if it were." The missiles would announce their presence, but their engine would make them an easy target, scanner or otherwise.

Another alarm sounded, more urgent than the first. "Twenty seconds, Hyken."

Hyken bit his lip. The second missile bay still flashed yellow, but should have changed to green by now. Two missiles were recommended against that class of freighter, but one might do the job. The ship in the window grew larger with every second. He could make out features with the naked eye; a yellow snake was painted on its side. His finger hovered over the button.

"Ten seconds."

The button clicked beneath his finger and the floor shuddered once again. A single streak of light raced away from the Sentinel. Both pilots held their breath. A yellow ball burst to life in front of them. Hyken held up a hand to shield his eyes. It was gone as quickly as it appeared. The false image from the light danced across his vision as he blinked.

"Mostly destroyed, but lots of debris incoming," Alard said, his voice still thick with concern. He pulled the harness over his shoulder and clicked the straps into place.

Hyken was already strapped-in, but tightened his harness anyways. They waited.

Nothing happened for a long moment. Then vibrations nudged the ship. There was a clang of metal on metal. Most of the debris was small, tiny spinning shards silhouetted against the yellow planet below. They pelted the Sentinel like rain, a steady, harmless shower. Eventually the tumult stopped, and only then did Hyken relax. He let out a deep breath and grinned over at his co-pilot. "I bet you're awake now, if the coffee didn't do the job!"

Alard ignored him, still squinting out the window. Hyken followed his gaze and saw it too; there was another silhouette out there, shapeless and spinning toward them. Neither man moved, their eyes transfixed on the object. It hit the window softly, scraping against the glass and nearly coming to a stop. The cockpit hardly gave off any light, but it was enough for them to see. The object had no arms or legs, but its head was intact, brown eyes staring lifelessly. Its mouth twisted in a silent scream.

Alard jerked away from the body, unstrapping his harness and jumping to the back of the small cockpit. Something close to pain painted his face, and though his mouth was open and moving no words came out. Hyken forced himself to chuckle. "First time seeing a body, eh?"

He pulled his eyes from the window to look at Hyken. His voice was barely more than a whisper. "That's a child."

"Is it?" He squinted and saw that Alard was right. "Man or child, they all die just the same."

The co-pilot returned to his seat. He tapped the keys of his computer.

"What are you doing?" Hyken asked him, but he didn't respond. "Don't bother, it's not worth the energy."

Numbers flashed across the screen. Alard swiped a finger to move through the data. Finally he found what he wanted, his finger freezing in the air. Slowly he leaned back in his chair. He turned to Hyken. "Thirty-eight. We

19

just killed thirty-eight people."

Hyken snorted. "The sensor must be wrong. Those freighters aren't meant to hold more than a crew of four."

The boy flicked a switch, and spotlights bathed the area with light. Dozens of bodies tumbled through space in front of the ship. Several were obviously men, but more were the smaller frames of women or children. Most floated peacefully now, but one or two still twitched and spasmed in the unapologetic vacuum of space.

Alard gasped, but Hyken only blinked. "Huh. They must have refitted the ship to carry passengers instead of cargo."

Alard's face twisted in pain. "They were just trying to flee."

"They were trying to get through to harass the Exodus Fleet." Hyken unclasped his harness and stood. "My shift's done. Reload the missile bay, so we don't have to see all of this next time." He strode from the cockpit, leaving Alard to stare out the window alone.

Outside the Sentinel the bodies floated, cold and broken.

Chapter 2

Hyken's body knew exactly when to wake, disabling the wake-up alarm from the screen next to his bed before it triggered. He rose to stretch, both outstretched arms nearly touching the walls of his narrow room. Three crisp, white uniforms hung on pegs. He changed into one before exiting into the hallway.

The Sentinel was only as large as it needed to be, with two separate sleeping bunks and a common room in addition to the cockpit. One long hallway that ran along the ship like a spine connected it all, with the cockpit at one end and the common room at the other. A ladder in the middle of the hallway led to the small airlock above. Hyken reached the back of the ship in ten long steps, the door sliding open at his approach.

The common room was crammed with functionality:

a food station that dispensed meals at regular intervals; an armory wall with two bio guns and various bits of lightweight armor; an exercise station, next to the cleanliness room. Hyken relieved himself in the latter, and then stepped into the exercise station. Presently it was a completely empty corner, white and pristine, until he made a selection from the wall computer. A cycling machine rose from the floor, stopping at just the right height.

The screen in front of the machine guided his effort as he pedaled, until his heart rate reached the required level. He breathed heavily but did not sweat; perspiration had long since been removed in the genetics of Melisao humans. He glanced out a small window that showed the yellow planet they orbited. He wondered if the Praetari still perspired. Praetar was settled millennia ago, so there were thousands of years where the two people evolved separately. *They probably do perspire*, Hyken decided. Everything on Praetar was dirty; it was easy to picture grime sticking to their sweaty skin.

He pedaled dutifully for 30 minutes until the computer beeped. The machine disappeared into the floor, leaving him standing on wobbly feet. His muscles ached from the effort. Endurance or physical strength training were required every day, but it was easier when Hyken was younger. At least it felt that way.

He pulled one leg up behind him to stretch. It didn't bother him much; physical strength wasn't as important for a Sentinel pilot as it was for a soldier or peacekeeper down on the surface. But it still made him feel old. Like

Saria, the red giant at the center of their system, it was a reminder that everything eventually died.

After precisely ten minutes of stretching he went to the food station. It was nothing more than a box-shaped indentation in the wall, with three holes from which food dispensed. From the computer screen he selected coffee, and for a few moments there was a soft hum. Finally from one hole slid a pouch, made of a transparent material that showed the dark liquid within.

The end popped off and he took a pull, letting the bitter taste wash around in his mouth. It took his mind back to Melis, to the small home on the bit of land his father once owned. He allowed himself to savor the memory for only a moment before shaking it from his head. *It'll all be gone soon, in my lifetime or the next.* There was no use focusing on it, not when there was much to do in the future. They had to look forward.

Preparations would need to be made for his sons to leave. The Exodus Fleet already prepared to leave the system, and the next wave of evacuations would begin after Hyken's tour. Cairne and Jon would get priority on the second fleet, because of Hyken's service. The Emperor blessed those who proved their loyalty.

He thought of the freighters trying to slip past the blockade. The Praetari used children as weapons, he knew. A child could reach places an adult could not, and even a small vest of explosives could kill hundreds. What if they reached the Exodus Fleet, dense with civilians? *Maybe I should pull up the training videos*, he thought.

That would help Alard remember the importance of their mission.

Saria was now visible in the common room window. Filters in the glass allowed him to look directly at the red giant without danger. It looked angry, more than usual. Flares of plasma swirled away from its surface, curling back inward in impossible arcs, pulled by the magnetic field. The surface itself shimmered like half-molten glass. It certainly looked like it was dying.

It wouldn't happen all at once, he knew. Stars burned by fusing hydrogen into helium. Most hydrogen was gone from Saria's core, and it was burning what was left in the outer shell, causing the star to slowly expand, over millions of years, until all the fuel was depleted. This expansion would destroy Melis, which orbited closer to the star than the other planets. Once the hydrogen was depleted the star would collapse, eventually becoming dense and hot enough to fuse helium instead.

But by then the Empire would be long gone. Melis was already a few hundred or thousand years from being uninhabitable, and the Emperor didn't want to wait any longer. There were lush, fertile systems only a few light years away, with primitive biology that could be easily discarded.

Hyken trusted the Emperor's judgement, both in the exodus and siege of Praetar. The Exodus Fleet must be protected. The Melisao Empire had to survive. They had to look forward.

With half his coffee gone he turned back to the

station to select a meal. Their options were limited, but he didn't mind. When he was younger he was bitter toward the Praetari, whom he assumed ate far better fare on the planet's surface than he did in orbit, but in his age he almost preferred the waxy, artificial food that was standard on Sentinel-class ships. There was a paralysis in having too many options, he'd found. Life was simpler when you didn't need to make such mundane decisions.

His finger froze before touching the computer. Both pilots were listed on the screen, with the number of meals they needed to consume during their shift. Hyken frowned at the screen before exiting the common room.

The cockpit door opened at his motion, giving Hyken a view of the yellow planet through the window. Alard sat in his chair, watching a video on the computer. There was the Emperor's face, solemn and determined as he spoke. "...will lead the way from the system, paving our path to a new Empire. Though our star becomes unstable, we will not. We must look forward."

Hyken recognized the speech from a few years before, when the first preparations were made to leave the system.

Alard didn't look up at his entrance, so Hyken sat in the other chair. Only when the video ended did he speak. "It's good to reaffirm yourself with the Emperor's words. I find myself doing it occasionally, when my shift grows long and boring."

The boy only nodded, not taking his eyes from the now blank screen. Outside the cockpit window an electroid moved, still cleaning debris and remains away from the ship. Hyken watched the human-shaped robot move silently through space to the other side of the ship before disappearing out of view.

"You missed your last two meals," Hyken finally said.

"I'm not hungry."

"It's not your decision. Eating is one of your duties."

He still didn't respond, or face him. Hyken could have ordered him to eat, but he knew there was no use. Not when there was something deeper bothering the boy. "That freighter probably had hidden weapons on-board."

Alard turned to him and shook his head. "It didn't. I checked. There was no sign of any volatile material in the wreckage."

Hyken tossed his bulb of coffee roughly onto the controls in front of him, his anger rising. "I ordered you not to bother. It's a waste of the ship's energy."

"It seemed like a suggestion. If you meant it as an order you should have been clearer."

Hyken clenched his jaw, and Alard stared back defiantly. It was the first time the boy showed any backbone in their few days together.

He opened his mouth to reprimand him, but then red light painted the boy's face and the rest of the cockpit all at once. The alarm was painful in his ears. They both turned to their computer screens: another ship was leaving the planet, still just a tiny prick of light in the atmosphere below.

Despite the alarm Alard relaxed back into his chair. When he spoke his voice held the correct tone of subordination. "I'm sorry. I've been feeling ill. That's why I missed my meal, and why I haven't been myself."

Hyken softened. "Have you checked your vitals?"

"No, but I will as soon as my shift's over. You go ahead and eat your meal. I'll eat after taking care of this freighter."

Hyken considered that a moment before nodding. "See that you do." He stood and returned to the hall. The cockpit doors whirred closed behind him, dampening the sound of the alarm.

I ought to file a report, he thought. Insubordination couldn't be tolerated, even if the boy was ill. It wasn't uncommon among rookies. A mark on his record wouldn't hurt him too much, but should give him the reprimand he needed. He nodded to himself. He would write the report during his shift, when Alard was asleep.

He reached the common room and selected one of the meals from the screen, bringing the food station once again to life. He felt the familiar shudder as the ship released its missiles. He smiled. The boy was doing his duty. Hyken himself had been stubborn as a rookie, questioning every order until he was put in his place. It reminded him how important it was to mold the young pilot, to help him become the loyal citizen the Melisao Empire needed. He needed to be more than Alard's co-pilot: he needed to be his mentor.

He'd left his coffee in the cockpit, he realized. His feet carried him back up the hallway, but something made him pause. He stopped just short of the door and pressed himself against the wall to peer through the square window without activating the door sensor. The room inside still flashed from the alarm, and Alard's gaze was fixed on the front window. Hyken shifted some more so he could see it: the Praetari freighter leaving the planet, and the two missiles hurrying toward it.

Hyken tensed as he watched, but just before they reached their target Alard touched his screen. The missiles exploded, blinding his view of that small section of space. But the cockpit still flashed red, and the freighter's information was still displayed on the screen. Hyken squinted through the after-image of the explosion: there it was, a rectangular ship still racing away from the planet. Intact.

Alard had detonated the missiles manually.

He was letting the freighter escape.

Hyken watched, unbelieving, until the ship drifted out of view and the Sentinel's proximity alarm ceased. Only then did Alard finally stir from his seat. Hyken stepped forward to trigger the door and enter the cockpit.

He retrieved his coffee and said, more calmly than he felt, "You take care of that ship?"

"Oh yeah, no problems. The missiles bays are reloading, too." He smiled wanly.

The ease with which he lied infuriated Hyken. Only

with great effort did he nod and leave the cockpit without saying more.

How many ships have gotten through? he thought when he was back in the common room. His meal was ready, steaming inside the food station, but he only stared at it while his mind raced. He'd never witnessed such defiance: both allowing the freighter to escape and manually detonating the missiles to hide it from his superior officer. It was treason.

He nearly marched back to the cockpit to confront him, but he made himself think it over. Was Alard acting on his own, or was it part of some larger conspiracy? There were separatists on Praetar, and elsewhere in the Empire. He pulled the name from memory: *Children of Saria.* Religious fanatics that worshiped the star and opposed the Empire's exodus. Alard's actions would make sense if he was one of the *Children*, he decided. Nobody could be that sympathetic toward Praetari without a deeper reason.

The boy didn't know he was aware. Perhaps Hyken's superiors would want to question him, to discover his true motives. The information would be valuable. He considered his options before deciding it wasn't a choice he could make on his own.

The food was cold in his mouth, but he chewed methodically while staring at the door, in the direction of the cockpit.

Alard was in a cheerful mood when he returned to the cockpit. Hyken forced himself to make small talk.

The boy smiled easily now, which was unsettling. He was downright pleased with himself, chatting eagerly about their tour and the Emperor's exodus plan. The facade twisted Hyken's stomach.

Finally the boy's shift ended, and Hyken watched him disappear down the hall and into the common room. He returned to his chair and pulled up the messaging system on the computer, typing quickly. Within moments the message was away to his commanding officer.

A thought occurred to Hyken. He should have done it earlier, when he was in the common room. It was necessary, he decided. But he would need to wait for Alard.

He returned to the door. He waited there, looking sideways out the window while staying out of view, for what seemed like an eternity. His legs tensed, still sore from his exercise. He strained his ears. The only sound was the hum of the ship's air recycler.

Finally the common room opened and Alard appeared. A bowl of food was in his hand; he ate eagerly, still looking pleased. He disappeared into his room. Hyken watched for several minutes until he was certain it was safe.

He left the cockpit, grateful for the soft shoes that muffled his steps. He slowed as he passed Alard's door, which had no window to reveal him. Inside the common room he went to the food station and turned around. He waited there a long moment, straining to hear anything.

When he was sure Alard wouldn't appear he stepped in front of the armory wall.

The gun was tiny, smaller even than his open palm. He hefted its weight. Sentinel pilots went through basic arms training, but that was a long time ago, and the cold material felt foreign against his skin. It was a biomass weapon, only deadly to lifeforms; it would cause no damage to the hull if fired.

He stuffed it inside his pocket and whirled, but he was still alone in the room. You need to relax, he told himself. He felt like a recruit, jittery and afraid. He needed direction, some orders to calm him down.

Back in the cockpit a small portion of the computer screen blinked. He tapped it and read the words:

Message received. Peacekeepers and replacement co-pilot will arrive in 10 hours. Observe delinquent but do not alert him. Use force only if strictly necessary.

He read the message three times, until it was memorized, before deleting it. He'd hoped for more definitive instructions on what to do. His options were limited. The Sentinel was a simple ship with no locks on the doors. He didn't think there was any way to confine Alard to his room. He could tie the boy up with a spare uniform, but that would do a poor job of holding him until the replacement arrived.

No, he wasn't supposed to alert him. He was only to

observe. That made no sense, but it was what he was ordered to do.

His ears pricked, and he leapt to the doorway. The door whirred open but the hallway was empty. The only noise was the soft purring of the ship. He fingered the gun in his pocket before returning to his chair. He took a deep breath, forcing himself to relax.

Hyken's shift was twelve hours. The reinforcements would arrive before then, while Alard still slept. If he was lucky he need not do anything. The gun felt heavy in his pocket.

The yellow planet stared back at him as he nodded to himself. He was a veteran of the Empire. He could handle a rookie for a few hours.

Chapter 3

It was near the end of the shift when the cockpit door opened. Hyken spun, startled, and there was Alard in the doorway. Hyken forced himself to remain in his chair, calm. He nodded to the boy politely.

Alard took the other chair. One hand was in his pocket, but the other trembled while it held a bulb of water to his mouth. His eyes were red and tensed. *Maybe he is sick,* Hyken thought. He glanced at the clock: there were two more hours until the peacekeepers arrived.

He forced a smile. "It was a quiet shift. No other souls to speak of."

Alard stared out the window at the planet. Hyken studied his face for any belied emotion. He was brooding, it seemed, all cheerfulness from the previous shift gone. Could he know of his fate, that armed peacekeepers raced to their location to remove him? There was no way for him to know, but he appeared suspicious. He hadn't even glanced in Hyken's direction since he entered.

"You didn't eat," Alard said. He fiddled with the computer, checking various data about the Sentinel.

"I'll eat in a little while."

"You're supposed to eat now," Alard said, smiling. "Eating is one of your duties."

Hyken chewed his lip. Refusing to eat would alert the boy more, but he didn't want to leave him alone in the cockpit. *Observe delinquent but do not alert him.* Detaining Alard then and there would violate his orders. And after a full shift Hyken's bladder was too full to hold him for long.

There wasn't much danger in leaving Alard alone for a few moments, he decided. The cockpit doors couldn't lock, and even if they could there wasn't much mayhem he could cause before Hyken returned. The worst he could do was inaction, if another freighter appeared. Hyken could eat fast.

"You're right," he finally said, standing. Alard was watching him carefully now. Had he waited too long to decide? "Even veterans gets stubborn every once in a while." He chuckled to himself, but his was the only laugh that echoed in the cockpit. He felt like running, but left the room in calm, calculated strides.

He emptied his bladder in the cleanliness room first,

then chose a meal from the food station. The machine was miserly with its food, but a pilot could have as much coffee as he wanted. He'd had four servings during his shift, he saw. *Too much. You're jittery, that's all.* He pressed the button for water and a plastic bulb appeared. He took a long drink.

The water immediately made him feel better. He began to relax. If the alarm went off he could return to the cockpit to ensure protocol was followed, but otherwise he need only relax and wait for the peacekeepers to arrive. There didn't need to be any confrontation at all.

He wondered what would happen to Alard. The separatists on Melis were publicly executed, but his co-pilot would undoubtedly be interrogated first. The Empire didn't know the Children of Saria's size and strength on Praetar. Alard's knowledge would be valuable indeed. Hyken might even be rewarded for uncovering him.

He started to turn around, but his gaze stopped on the armory wall. He froze.

The second gun was missing.

Everything changed. His mind raced to think of new plans. For a long moment he didn't move, the water still held in his outstretched hand. The food dispensing from the station with a soft *thud* finally jolted him back to alertness.

The hallway was empty, but Hyken watched it from the doorway a long while, opening his eyes wide to take in every detail. He moved up the corridor, picking each step carefully as if on dangerous ground. He paused at Alard's room, slowly leaning his head around the doorway. The room was empty. He continued up the hall, the only noise the soft wheezing from his breath. The gun seemed heavier in his pocket, pulling against his uniform.

Hyken reached the cockpit door, Alard still unmoved from his chair. The door made a soft sound as it opened, but Alard still didn't take his gaze from the planet. The back of his head was visible, but the chair blocked his view of the rest of him. He couldn't see his hands.

He reached inside his pocket. The gun felt cool to the touch. He could do it right then, without Alard ever turning around. It wouldn't be a violation of his orders, now that the boy posed a real threat. The ship logs would confirm he took the gun. Alard's knowledge was valuable, but not worth dying over. Hyken's grip tightened on his weapon.

Just then Alard stood. With both hands in his pockets he regarded Hyken with red, puffy eyes. He leaned against the wall. His hands were still hidden.

Hyken tensed in the doorway. The opportunity was gone, but he didn't loosen the grip on his gun. He thought he could shoot first, but it was still risky. *I just need to buy a little time for the peacekeepers to arrive.*

His mind worked quickly as he stepped into the cockpit. "Yesterday you said you only wanted to do one tour. What would you do when you're done? As a civilian?"

It was such an unexpected question that Alard looked surprised. He considered for a moment. "I've always wanted to do construction," he said, his eyes brightening. "Any sort of building: homes or offices, or places where people can go to eat. They'll need builders, wherever the Fleet settles. That's sort of like creating life, I suppose, but with bricks instead of genetics."

"That's not the same as having children," Hyken said, trying to extend the conversation. "Not the same by far. A house can never laugh with you, an office never play in the rain and grow before your eyes."

"Maybe not, but it's what I would enjoy doing."

Silence returned to the cockpit, and the two men regarded one-another warily. Hyken knew he looked awkward standing there, but he didn't want to sit. He tried to think of something else to say, anything to fill the time, but Alard spoke first.

"Tell me about your children."

It caught Hyken off guard, but he was glad for it. He could talk about his boys for hours. "What do you want to know?"

"I don't know. What was your last memory of them?"

Alard didn't want to shoot him, Hyken realized. He was looking for an excuse not to. Whatever the boy's treasonous motivations, he wasn't resolved.

He thought of a story, not of the last time he saw his children, but one that was better suited just then. "I took them to one of the local parks on Melis, after returning from my last tour. It was a fine day, warmer than most, and we didn't need to bundle up. We were scouting through the woods and heard a noise. Jon races ahead to see what it was. There was a hound, a stray by the look of its fur, hiding against a tree. The coyotes had gotten to it, and its legs were all mangled and torn. It made a terrible noise. My boys cried at the sight. I had to send them away so I could put it down. We went home after that, the boys were so disturbed. It ruined the day."

Alard listened intently, his hands still in his pockets.

Hyken thought he had him. "There's too much death in these worlds, Alard. Life is too precious to waste needlessly."

Alard's eyes widened, suddenly fervent. "Exactly! Death should be avoided wherever possible. If there's a way to save lives, it should be done no matter what the cost."

Shit, Hyken thought. His words had the opposite effect. The boy was frowning out the window at Praetar, and his hands seemed to move within the pocket. Hyken considered talking to him more, but instead he sighed.

"Why did you take the gun, Alard?"

He looked back, determined now. "Why did *you?*"

Neither man moved for a long moment. Hyken's hand tightened on the gun in his pocket. Even if the boy drew first he wouldn't shoot, he thought. There was no other choice then. Hyken started to draw his gun.

The familiar alarm screamed, flashing the cockpit red.

Alard's head jerked to the screen. There was Hyken's chance to shoot, to end the threat. But years of muscle memory and habit took over. He jumped to the computer, bending to the controls to pull up the information. It was another Praetari freighter, even more underweight than the others.

"Stop!" Alard said. He pointed the gun with two shaky hands.

Hyken turned to face him, holding out his hands. "Put the gun away. We have a job to do."

"They're just civilians."

"They're a threat."

"No they're not!" Alard's face was paler than his uniform. "Every ship I've scanned has been full of civilians. No weapons at all."

"You don't understand," Hyken yelled above the alarm. "It's not our job to pick and choose. It's our job to follow our orders."

"An electroid could pilot a Sentinel if that's all they wanted. They send two of us so choices like this can be made." He was pleading then.

"You may have had a point before you disobeyed orders, hid it from your commanding officer, and then pointed a weapon at him." Hyken turned back to the computer and typed. The Praetari freighter zoomed larger on the screen. A red snake was painted on its hull. It tilted toward them.

"I'll shoot you." The voice was soft, barely audible through the pulsing alarm.

"You've never pointed a gun at anyone," Hyken said, not moving from the computer. He tapped at the screen and the Sentinel's weapons locked onto the freighter. "Even if you could shoot me, what's your plan? Kill me and fly off, until the empire hunts you and the other *Children* down?"

Confusion spread on Alard's face. "What?" The weapon shook in his hands.

He would have shot me already, if he could. "Just put the gun down and let me do my job. There's nothing to be gained by doing this."

"I can save them." Alard's voice quavered. His eyes were wide and hopeful.

"You would threaten one of your own to save a ship full of foreigners?"

Alard shook his head. "I'm nothing like you. You're a murderer."

Hyken snarled and smashed a key with his palm, and the missiles zoomed away.

Alard turned to the screen, horrified. One hand shot out to the controls. Hyken lunged, knocking him sideways into the wall, but it was too late. Orange and yellow flames illuminated the cockpit as the missiles detonated, well short of their target. Hyken screamed his fury at the boy's intervention, and again charged into him.

They fell to the floor together, a jumble of thrashing arms. Hyken landed on top and punched at his head, knocking it back into the floor. Through the alarm's siren he heard the gun clatter across the room. Alard clawed around with his hand, searching for it, but Hyken continued to pummel him, knocking him into the floor again and again. Slowly the boy's protests grew weaker.

Hyken heaved one final blow and fell backward against the base of his chair. His co-pilot was motionless, his face a mess of bloody bits. He watched him for several moments before deciding he was unconscious. He could still salvage his mission.

His hands throbbed. It felt like his knuckles were broken. He must have taken some blows himself, because the side of his face felt like it was on fire. With a groan he pulled himself to his feet.

The Praetari ship continued on, still far from the Sentinel. *Should have enough time*, he thought, beginning the missile reloading sequence.

There was a noise behind him; he turned to see Alard standing. His eyes were islands of white in a sea of red. He whimpered as he raised his weapon. Hyken fumbled, pulling his own gun from his pocket.

A single blast echoed through the cockpit, and only the sound of the Sentinel's alarm remained.

Tales of a Dying Star

Part II: The Mother

Tales of a Dying Star

Chapter 4

The sharp corner of the electroid part cut Mira's finger, and blood dripped along the conveyor belt at her station. *Stars no*, she thought, frantically wiping the finger on her soiled shirt. With her other sleeve she rubbed at the bloodied robot part, shiny and with exposed wires at both ends, but her effort only smeared red across the chrome. She tried again on two more stained parts but they fared no better. With horror she watched them roll away from her station.

She returned to her work, fastening protective plating to the electronics and tightening them with bolts. A certain amount of defective parts were expected to get through, and would be summarily discarded, but they would be tallied against Mira's record. She was already in poor standing with the factory foreman. Their factory produced electroids, the robot workers that could be used to replace any manner of human activity. Electroid laborers made no mistakes, but the robots built in the factory were needed in a different part of the solar system, so the assembly line work fell to humans. Besides, why make electroids build more electroids when there were so many workers on Praetar, desperate to earn their food?

The parts came from three large openings along one wall, snaking through the room along the conveyor belt before exiting at the other end. Mira connected two more metal pieces together while cradling her cut finger, and in the few seconds she had between parts she clutched her hand to her shirt, silently willing the blood to clot. Even then her hand still trembled. Whether it was from fear or exhaustion or malnutrition she didn't know, but the tremble had lasted three days and showed no sign of stopping. She dared not tell the foreman, not when she was so close to saving enough food credits to leave. She glanced at the foreman's office, a room at the center of one wall with a huge window to observe the factory floor. The windows were tinted just then, the foreman busy at some task.

Farther down the conveyor belt Elena cursed, tossing down an electroid part in disgust. She looked up the line at Mira and made a rude gesture with her hand. Mira bent back to her work to ignore her. The fear bubbled up then, rising from her aching chest and simmering at the back of her throat. Even if the tally of mistakes did not cost Mira her job, Elena would surely complain. She had the foreman's ear in a way the others did not; several women had been removed at her behest. Mira pushed the fear away and continued assembling the electroid parts that rolled in front of her, because there was nothing else for her to do.

The entrance to the factory was on the wall opposite the foreman's office. Mira whipped her head toward it as the doors opened, exposing the dim room to daylight. Two peacekeepers entered side-by-side, each with an electronic gun spiraling down their right arm. A red light blinked on each weapon, signaling their intent.

Mira's eyes whipped back to her station, as if avoiding eye-contact could somehow save her. *No, please no*, she thought, saying a silent prayer to the stars. She'd worked so hard, was so close. *They can't take me, not now. I've worked so hard. Kaela and Ami need me.*

She watched out of the corner of her eye as they walked along the wall. A whimper escaped her cracked lips. Their footsteps on the factory floor grew louder as they approached. Nausea and dread grew until she thought she might vomit or collapse.

They arrived at her station and continued past, never looking in her direction.

Mira sighed as they reached another station, their boots clicking to a stop in front of a scrawny woman with rough hair. The woman screamed then, and took a step backward as if to run, but the peacekeepers raised their weapons and she collapsed to the floor in terror. She curled up into a ball and began howling, her chest shaking in violent sobs. The men were forced to drag her across the floor, each one holding an arm. She kicked like a child, but had neither the strength or courage to pose any true threat. When the door to the factory closed only darkness remained, and the soft hum of the belt.

Elena watched it all with satisfaction. She shot a smug look at Mira before returning to her work.

Mira felt guilty at being relieved, but it only lasted a moment. She didn't know the woman that was taken, but wouldn't trade places with her for anything on Praetar.

It was the last day of the week, according to the Melisao calendar, so when their shift ended the hundred women lined up at the foreman's office. None of them talked; there were no friends there, and they were too exhausted, besides.

The line crept forward until Mira finally stood at the foreman's desk. Jin was bald and stocky, with crystal blue eyes that were foreign on Praetar. They would have been attractive, Mira thought idly, if they'd held any warmth. He was flanked on either side by guards, should the workers become unruly while receiving their pay.

"Mira, age twenty-three, two children," he read from the computer screen. He inspected her with his eyes, as if searching for some flaw. He must have found none, for he pulled his gaze away and opened a drawer. Grooves held rows of glass discs inside, each the size of a fingernail. Jin removed a full row and counted out twenty-one discs on the desk, arranging them in three neat stacks. He closed the drawer and looked at her again, and only after a long moment did he finally say,

"You may go."

She scooped up the food credits and stuffed them into her pocket before fleeing the office. Elena still waited in line; Mira felt the woman's eyes as she walked by. She still had her job, though she did not know for how long.

The air outside was almost as acrid as the factory. Somewhere above the sun still shined, but the thick clouds that enveloped Praetar blocked most of its light, leaving a yellowish haze across the planet. The Melisao complained about it, but Mira couldn't imagine any other landscape.

There was only one city on Praetar, spread along a tiny strip of land between the sulphuric oceans and the desert. She gazed south, toward the tall dunes of sand. The desert people survived out there, somehow. She didn't understand how, without food or water. Not to mention the long, coiling monsters that slithered under the sand. But more Praetari wandered into the desert every day, looking for an escape from the Melisao occupation. It would have been tempting if not for her daughters.

One long street ran along the city like a spine, stretching away from the factory in either direction. Mira turned right, picking her steps carefully to avoid cutting her bare feet on the debris scattered across the dirt.

A pair of boys armed with pieces of metal stood at the edge of an alley. They stopped their conversation to watch her. She quickened her step along the pavement, keeping her head down and watching them at the edge of her vision, ready to bolt. On pay days she usually needed to run home, but today she wasn't sure if her legs had the strength. To her relief the boys made no move.

Her feet ached by the time she reached the market only six blocks away. It was a true market once, with stalls of every kind of food and good for sale. But ever since the Melisao came it was a place for them to dispense a trickle of food to the populace: thick bread, thin soup, and strips of manufactured meat.

Again she waited in line. When she reached the front the peacekeeper stared at her implacably from behind a tinted helmet. His uniform was white, pristine. She pointed to the container of bread and held up three fingers and pulled three credits from her pocket. She agonized over the discs in her trembling hand, so small and precious, before returning one to her pocket. The others she dropped onto the countertop. Only then did the soldier place two cylinder-shaped loaves in front of her. He quickly pulled his hand back, as if afraid her touch might soil his uniform.

She walked for another hour with the bread clutched to her chest. It was dark by the time she reached a nine-floored building at the edge of town. It was a shell of a structure, grey and bleak and half-destroyed from the invasion. It leaned ever so slightly, as if it might collapse at any moment. A few children played in the street, and three women with colorful face makeup sat on the curb. The children begged Mira for food, but the women only watched her walk inside. Mira's feet carried her up the cement stairs to the fourth floor, to the small room that belonged to her.

"Mama!" her girls cried when she entered, wrapping themselves around her legs. They were smaller than they should be for their age, with thin, brittle hair. She held them tight, saying a silent prayer that they had stayed safe, as she did whenever she returned from the factory. Ami was still too young to wander far, but Kaela was seven and grew more restless every day. Mira feared she would disobey her and venture outside.

Their room would have been cramped for just one person with barely enough room to lay flat on the floor. The walls were made of the same yellow, flakey bricks that most of Praetar was built with. A layer of dust covered the floor. The room had the remains of a window that gave a view of the street below and the hazy sky above.

She broke one of the loaves in half, then into fourths, and gave each girl a piece. "Eat it slowly," she warned, but the girls sat on the floor and tore into it eagerly. Ami wheezed between bites.

Mira was too weary to stop them. Instead she went to the corner where they slept. She knelt at the wall and removed a square of loose stone, revealing a cubby hole just large enough for the square box inside. She slid it out and emptied her pockets, adding the nineteen credits to the collection, which now filled half the box. She took care not to make any noise. *A few more weeks*, she thought, before returning the box to the hole and

51

replacing the stone.

She joined her daughters on the floor and ate her own piece of bread, taking small bites to make the meal last longer. It was hard, nutritionally dense and flavorless, but when she was done she eyed the remaining piece. She placed it and the second loaf on the jutting brick that served as a shelf, above the girls' reach, to keep herself from looking at it too long.

"Tell us a story," Kaela said, curling up in the corner.

"Which one do you want to hear?" Mira asked. She sat back down with her back against the wall. "How about Oasis, the paradise in the sky we'll one day visit?"

"I want to... hear about... Big Father Zitro... fighting the striped monsters." The words came out slowly, as Ami needed to pause to breathe between every few words. Mira cringed at how weak she sounded, but forced a smile.

They'd heard the story a hundred times, but Mira told it again anyway. The girls were snoring softly by the time Zitro scared away the monsters with his club. She laid them down underneath their blankets and joined them, and stared at the loose rock covering her hiding place until she too fell asleep.

Chapter 5

Mira felt the coughs before she heard them. She opened her eyes to find Ami convulsing violently under their blanket. Darkness still showed through the broken window above them.

Kaela was already awake, kneeling over her little sister. "Mama? What's wrong?"

She threw the blankets off and turned Ami over. Her face was a terrible shade of red. Her cheeks puffed out as the coughs came deep from within her lungs. Normally Mira would smooth her daughter's hair and sing to her softly until the spasms passed, but this was worse than usual. She wheezed in between fits, her chest heaving with false-breaths. Scared, bloodshot eyes stared up at her mother. *She can't breathe.*

"What's wrong?" Kaela repeated, mirroring their fear.

"Everything's fine," Mira said, but her voice gave her away. Kaela's eyes widened. "Stay here. I'll return soon." She scooped Ami into her arms and carried her from the building.

Even at night the yellow haze was thick in the air, illuminated by the street lamps that somehow weren't destroyed in the invasion. The low clouds seemed to reflect it back down, giving the city a constant semblance of twilight. The clouds reflected blue and green to the west though, which was the direction Mira ran.

A gang of six boys laughed at one-another from an open alley, watching with curiosity as she passed. Her daughter was heavy enough that Mira couldn't move fast. The heels of her feet ached almost immediately. Ignoring the pain she continued on past row after row of broken apartments and factories. Ami made pitiful noises from her arms, urging Mira faster.

She reached the Station after only a few minutes. The Station was one central building surrounded by a scattering of smaller square-shaped huts erected after the occupation, so named because it was a terminal for ground and air transportation before the occupation. Now, it was claimed by Bruno and his men, and for whatever reason the Melisao allowed it. Signs glowing in bright colors advertised food and drink and every manner of illicit activity. The steady pumping of music drifted out from the main building.

Mira approached the open gate along a haphazard fence of interlocking metal surrounding the Station. Four guards wearing bits of leather and chain were on duty. She kept her head down to avoid stirring their boredom. Two held only clubs, but the others had guns, and raised them slightly at her approach. Once she was through she quickened her step again.

The room she sought was in the central building. Lights swirled and spun inside the entrance hallway, blinding her with alternating shades of blue and red and green. The music was deafening. People crowded the hall dancing, and Mira held her daughter close. Two women with white legs and colorful makeup writhed against one-another, sneering as Mira passed.

At the end of the hallway was a huge steel door, rimmed with bolts the size of her fist. Mira stopped at a door before then, this one smaller and marked with an innocent blue X. She banged on it with her palm. When nobody answered she banged again, more desperate this time. The people dancing in the hallway shot annoyed looks at her, but she didn't care. Ami still whimpered in her arms.

She was about to knock a third time when the door finally opened, only a crack. Half a face was visible, one eye searching around before finally settling on Mira.

"Huh?" was all he said.

Mira held up Ami, and poured all her desperation into her voice. "My daughter is sick. Please, *help me.*"

The doctor looked at them a moment longer before slamming the door closed.

Mira gaped. She stared at the door, wondering if she should knock and plead some more. She looked around the hallway to see if anyone might help, but everyone ignored her, intent on their own activities. She glanced at the big door at the end of the hall. If she went to Bruno for help, what would he say? Worse, what would his price be?

But then several locks clicked and the doctor's door opened. He pulled them inside and swung it shut, not bothering to lock it behind them.

He was bare from the waist up, with a yellow tail of hair running down an otherwise bald head. The thinness of his chest and limbs hinted at addiction, with a sunken look to his eyes. "How long has she been like this?" he asked, taking Ami from her arms.

"Less than an hour. She woke like this, in the night."

Mira looked around the room, which was cluttered with dirty boxes and crates. Along one wall was a wooden bed piled with blankets, with a colorful woman on her back, passed out. The opposite wall was tidy, with pristine counters and cabinets that still held unbroken glass, showing neat rows of jars and vials behind.

In the center of the room was an examination table on which the doctor laid Ami. He reached above and flicked a light that hung from the low ceiling. "Not like this. How long has she had the cough altogether? A week? Two?"

"A month," she admitted.

"She should have been brought here sooner." He shook his head and prodded the child's temple with his fingers.

"We didn't have the credits," Mira said. Ami stared up at the doctor's unfamiliar face and began to kick and wheeze. Mira held her hand. "It was never bad until tonight."

"You have the credits now, I hope," he said, still focused on her daughter. "She needs medicine to open her airway or she won't survive the night."

"How many?"

"Five credits for my time, and fifty for the medicine."

Mira's heart sank. That was more than half her savings. Still, there was no decision to make. She answered immediately. "Agreed. I'll return with them in the morning."

The doctor looked up from the table and barked a laugh. "If I had a credit for every time someone *promised* me payment, I'd be richer than Bruno. You'll bring the credits now, or you'd better fetch the priest instead."

Mira stared at Ami agonizingly, and her own throat constricted. "You would let her die here, in front of you?"

"I don't know you," he said, putting his hands up, "and I can't risk myself for a stranger."

If he was sorry he showed no sign. Mira quickly kissed Ami on the forehead and whispered, "I'll be back," before running from the office.

The guards at the fence heckled her as she left the compound, but she had no ears for them. She ran down the street until her breath was ragged and her feet throbbed, past the gang of boys and upstairs to her room.

Kaela whimpered in the corner, her eyes widening when her mother burst through the door. "Where's... where's Ami?"

"Everything's okay," she said, throwing aside the rock from the corner. She didn't bother counting out the 55 credits instead clutching the entire box to her chest as she left.

She took the stairs two-at-a-time and rounded the entrance to the street–and tripped over something, sending the box hurtling through the air. Her wrists took most of the impact, but not all, and when her head hit the pavement she saw spots of yellow and white. The box clattered across the street, but thankfully remained intact.

When her vision returned Mira pushed to her knees, but a foot between her shoulder blades pressed her back to the ground.

"You in a hurry," said one of the boys. She could see several pairs of feet around her. She twisted her head to face the one who spoke. His red hair fell to his shoulder in curls, and his face was blotched with pimples. He was stout, more than any boy on Praetar ought to be.

"She dropped this," said another, picking up the box. The glass inside clinked as he shook it. He turned the box over and opened the lid. His eyes grew wide.

The others gathered around. Someone whistled. "Where'd she get all the glass?"

"She must be a whore."

"Doesn't look like any whore I ever seen. No makeup or nothing."

The stout boy said, "She must be a thief." He spat on the ground by Mira's face, which was still pressed against the dirty pavement. "This is our block. She outta know that. Might be we should show her so." His feet turned to face her. Mira clenched her eyes shut.

"We could buy a lot of *plourine* at the Station."

"I wanna buy a girl."

The stout boy turned back to face the others. "You ain't doin' nothin' with it til we take it to the Station. If she stole it Bruno'd want to know. He'll *reward* us."

"I picked it up, I oughta spend some. Bruno won't know."

"I said no."

Mira heard a thud as one of the boys cried out. She twisted and watched the two scuffle, their arms wrapped around one-another as they wrestled to the ground. The boy holding the box stood over them, paralyzed, unsure of whether to join in or keep watching.

He was about the same size as Mira.

Desperation making her brave, Mira jumped to her feet with newfound strength. She slammed her shoulder into the boy and grabbed the box from his arms as he fell backwards. Then she was away, sprinting down the street before he hit the ground. Her feet throbbed again but she didn't care. Mira ran as if her own life depended on it, not just Ami's.

She didn't know if the boys followed because she never slowed enough to check.

She was sweaty and breathing fast when she reached the Station. This time the guards were too confused to leer as she ran past. She must have looked determined because the dancers in the hallway stepped out of her way too. She burst into the doctor's office.

The room was dark, the examination table empty.

Oh stars, am I too late? Confusion and panic and anger welled-up, until movement at the edge of the room caught her eye. She whirled; there was the doctor and the woman who was passed out, sitting on the edge of the bed. In the woman's arms was Ami, giggling while the woman stuck her tongue out and made faces at her.

"I gave her the medicine," the doctor said. He was suddenly sheepish.

"Star shit, Leo," the woman said, "you were keen to do nothing until I made you treat her. Stubborn oaf."

Mira pulled Ami to her chest with one arm, squeezing until the girl squeaked. "Mom, you're hurting me!" she said with a giggle as if nothing was wrong.

The woman stood. The makeup around her eyes was bright pink, with three green slashes that trailed back toward her ears. "Such a precious girl, too. I told Leo I'd cover the cost and make you come work with me if you couldn't pay. You're a pretty one, with that yellow hair." It seemed like half a joke, but she eyed Mira up and down until fixing her gaze on the box under Mira's arm.

"Oh I have the credits," she said, placing the box on the table and opening it for them to see.

The woman frowned, almost disappointed.

The doctor went to the clean side of the room, opened a drawer, and returned with a packet of needles. "She needs a shot every night before she sleeps, to keep her airway open. It will help for a few weeks, maybe."

Mira frowned. "Only a few weeks? This won't cure her?"

"What she needs is fresh air." He laughed, but neither woman joined him. "Look, her lungs are weak from breathing this crud. The shots will help strengthen them, but it won't last forever."

Mira paid him and said farewell to the prostitute. When she pulled the box under one arm it was agonizingly light. "Make sure she eats more!" he called as she left the Station.

She would need to take the longer route home to avoid the gang. By then it would almost be morning. Ami was cheerful and talkative in her arms, the fearful night already forgotten. Mira put on a brave face, but as soon as her daughter fell asleep she began to cry.

Chapter 6

The conveyor belt hummed as Mira worked. Her hands seemed to move of their own accord, without their usual trembling, and she found herself in a good rhythm that day. Perhaps the lack of sleep aided her, exhausting her enough that she hadn't the energy to falter, counterintuitive as that may seem. Or maybe she was resigned to the fact that she would stand at that conveyor belt until she, or the red giant Saria, were dead. Whatever the reason, her hands fastened the electroid parts together deftly.

The star may not even die before we do, she thought, glancing to the factory doors where a hint of sunlight shone through the cracks. She didn't understand how it would happen, but the Emperor was leaving the system with urgency, so perhaps he knew something the rest of them didn't.

There was another way. A way that could give her daughters a life not covered in a thin yellow haze. It had fueled Mira's hope every day. But that hope was gone now, or so far out of reach that it made no difference. It would be months before she could save up enough credits now. Ami's medicine wouldn't last that long. Mira hadn't fallen so low as to cover her face in makeup and work at the Station, but her desperation grew greater every day.

At least Ami was healthy, however short it might last. She was completely unphased by the events of the night, and even wanted to stay awake to play with her older sister when they returned home early that morning. Kaela was exhausted though; Mira thought she cried the whole time they were gone. However carefree Ami might be, her sister was old enough to understand they were in trouble. If only they were all as unburdened as the two-year-old.

The speakers overhead crackled with static. The voice that spoke seemed hollow, more machine than human. "Mira, report to the foreman's office."

She froze at her station, holding two electroid parts above the conveyor belt. She listened, waiting for the message to repeat itself. The voice was hardly clear, so perhaps she had misheard. But no, somebody coughed politely behind her. When Mira turned she saw Angela standing there, the replacement worker that roamed the factory and took women's place when they needed to use the toilet. Mira handed over the parts and left her station.

If they wanted to remove me it would have been yesterday, she thought. That was what they usually did, waiting until the last day so they wouldn't need to pay for the week's work. *Maybe Jin just wants to give me a warning.* She'd let plenty of electroid parts get through unfinished when her hand was trembling, so it would come as no surprise if she were reprimanded.

Maybe he wanted something else. Elena bragged that she knew how to please Jin, but he might be bored with her. Mira was handsome, at least when she had a chance to clean the grime from her face. Perhaps that was why he wanted to see her. The thought made her nauseous. She considered turning around and fleeing the factory altogether, but somehow she kept walking forward.

Women glanced up from their work as she passed. Mira saw expressions of fear, or sympathy, or relief. She didn't look back at any of them, except Elena, whose face she searched for clues of what awaited. But her face only held curiosity, not the smug satisfaction of responsibility. Elena had not caused her fate, whatever it may be.

The anteroom to the foreman's office was where his secretary sat, a prim-looking woman with tight hair and legs as white as the women at the Station. Jin the Foreman was bent over her desk, speaking to her quietly. "Go on in, I'll be there in a moment," he said when he finally noticed Mira standing there.

His office had a tall window facing the factory floor. Many of the workers stared openly now, eager to observe her fate. She felt like an animal on display. The only chair was the one behind the desk, so she shuffled to the corner next to the window, where she could not be seen through the glass. She felt foolish, but a little less afraid.

She saw it then, just visible from around the edge of the desk. The top drawer was open slightly, and the light overhead reflected off rows of glass. She didn't know how many credits were there, but it was more than she'd ever seen.

Why would he leave the drawer unlocked and open? Was it a trap? She knew the Melisao played games with the Praetari, baiting them into breaking the law so they could make an example. There had to be thousands of credits there, more than she would earn in a lifetime.

Jin entered the room then, closing the door behind him with a click. He jerked when he realized she was in the corner. He eyed her suspiciously as he went around his desk, lowering himself slowly into the chair. He clicked a button on his desk and the window darkened slightly. "I don't blame you for hiding," Jin said, "you women are vicious to one another. You can relax now; they cannot see you."

He seemed oblivious to the open drawer next to him, showing no sign that he knew Mira had been looking at it. He took her silence for agreement and nodded to himself.

She took a step toward the desk. "You wanted to see me?"

"Your daughter was sick last night."

Mira opened her mouth, but then closed it again. How could he possibly know? Was she being spied on, or followed? If he knew Ami was sick he probably knew they'd been to the Station, a place all workers were warned to avoid.

Her fear must have been obvious, for he quickly said, "I have a child back home too. I'll have another, after this tour."

Mira didn't know what that meant, but she nodded.

Jin reached into the open drawer, pulling out a handful of glass. The credits clinked three times as he stacked them on the table.

Jin's blue eyes watched her without expression. Was he waiting for a reaction? Was this a test, like the open drawer? Did he want her to beg, or worse, did he want something in return?

"She'll have quite the hunger, if she's anything like mine after an illness," he said. He nudged the three credits forward a bit. "This will help set her right, I hope."

Mira stepped forward, still cautious of a trap, before scooping up the credits. "Thank you," she managed to squeak, lowering her eyes to the floor.

Jin waved a hand. "Just don't tell the others. I have a few extra credits I can dispense without getting in trouble, but I don't want the whole factory crying to me with stories of their sick children. You may go." He tapped at his computer screen, his attention already elsewhere.

Angela didn't bother to conceal her surprise that she returned from the foreman's office, but Mira didn't begrudge her. She was still surprised, herself. The rest of the day went by quickly, with her mind a mixture of confusion and guilt.

Her daughters were excited to see her that night, crying out with surprise when she revealed the bowl of soup she bought on the way home. It was thin and mostly water, but they sat on the floor around the bowl and ate eagerly, dipping the tough bread and taking turns sipping from the spoon.

When their meal was complete and another bedtime story had been told, Mira took the medicine from the shelf. She held Ami close, whispering soothing words into her ear as she pressed the needle into her chest. Her daughter sat perfectly still through it all, brave for a girl her age.

"Am I fixed?"

Her voice was hopeful. Mira forced a smile. "You were never broken, sweet girl."

Chapter 7

The foreman sat behind the glass of his office, staring idly at his computer screen as he did every morning. He held a drink in his hand, some red liquid that came from an exotic fruit Mira had never seen. She tried to imagine what it must taste like, and decided it was probably tart. She'd had a tart fruit once, when she was very young. She smacked her lips involuntarily. Her mind remembered the taste, even if her tongue did not.

He hadn't moved all morning, but Mira knew that was normal. She'd observed him for two weeks and knew his routine by heart. It was a boring job, foreman of a factory: tap at the computer screen, watch the women through the window, occasionally reprimand one of them. Nothing of note ever happened, except for one thing, every third day, halfway through her shift. And today was the third day.

Mira had exhausted all other options. Leo didn't need an assistant in his office, and had laughed when she offered to sell her malnourished blood. She'd gone door-to-door in her building after that, offering to clean or watch children or any other small task that needed doing, but nobody needed help. Most cursed her for even asking. Trust was uncommon on Praetar these days.

Painting her face and working at the Station was still an option, but she wasn't that desperate. She would turn to thievery before that.

Ami's medicine was nearly used up; she didn't know how long the girl would stay healthy after it was gone. No, this was her best option. Mira worked steadily at her station, but glanced to the foreman's office every few heartbeats. Her plans were made, and today may be the only opportunity.

The electroid parts clicked together. Mira tightened them with a drill, the tips of her fingers throbbing where she'd pricked herself with a sewing needle. When she looked back up the foreman was no longer idle: his lips moved as he gestured and spoke to his computer screen. Mira stiffened. Two parts rolled past her station unassembled, but she didn't take her eyes from the office. Finally Jin stood, his conversation complete. He ran a hand over his bald head and began pacing behind the desk.

Soon, Mira thought. She forced herself to return to her work, this time glancing at the front door instead of the foreman's office. More electroid parts passed her station carelessly assembled, but she paid them no mind. Soon her record as a factory employee wouldn't matter.

It was not long before a shadow appeared through the cracks in the door. Blinding daylight filled the factory. The other women looked up from their stations, but Mira turned away from hers. She strode to where Angela sat, picking at her fingernails with a tiny bit of metal. "Take my station for a few minutes. I need to use the toilet."

Angela rolled her eyes as she stood, but Mira was already moving away. She took long strides across the factory floor, moving as fast as she could without raising suspicion. She saw them then, the three men who had entered. Their uniforms were not white like most peacekeepers, but the greasy black shade officers wore. They walked along the wall at a brisk pace, unspeaking, as if eager to be done with their task.

Mira passed the hallway where the cleanliness room were located but continued on. That was not her destination.

She reached Jin's office before they did. His secretary began a formal greeting, but gave a start when she saw it was Mira. The foreman came out of his office, and he too frowned when he saw Mira.

"Foreman," Mira said, "I need to speak with you."

"Now?" he asked. His face and neck were flushed.

"Yes. Please, it's important. It's about my daughter."

The three officers appeared in the doorway. The man in the middle was surprised to see Mira, regarding her with annoyance. For a long moment she feared Jin would scold her in front of the other Melisao, but instead he said, "Wait in my office." He led the three men back out to the factory floor.

Mira slipped inside the office and swung the door nearly shut behind her, enough to block the view inside. She waited for the foreman and his guests to walk past the window and out of sight, then pressed the button on the desk to tint the glass. It might arouse suspicion, but it was better for the other women to *suspect* than see her actual crime. Besides, she would be gone before any of them had a chance to complain to the foreman.

The officers always spent five minutes inspecting the factory. More than enough time.

She crossed the office and opened the drawer, the rows of discs clinking from the motion. She grabbed a handful and reached over her shoulder, sliding them down her back into the secret pocket sewn into the shirt between her shoulder blades. Mira counted the handfuls as her shirt grew heavy, not bothering to take an exact amount, until she was sure she had enough.

The drawer shut quietly, but as she turned to leave the secret pocket ripped from the weight. A trickle of credits slid down her back. Some caught in her pants but more fell to the floor with a clatter. She bent down and clutched at her back, stopping more from spilling.

She crouched there, frozen, waiting for the secretary

to burst inside and reveal her crime. But there was only silence, and the door remained closed.

Careful not to spill more, Mira slipped one arm inside her shirt and lifted it over her head while clutching the pocket closed with the other. Now bare-chested, she examined the seam. The stitching had come loose at the corner of the pocket, revealing a hole just large enough to let the discs slip out. She tightened the thread with her finger to close the gap, but it wouldn't stay closed by itself.

She pulled a needle and thread from her pants and began the repair. Her hand still trembled; it took several attempts just to make the first stitch. The second stitch took just as long. Panic made her chest ache, and it seemed like an eternity before the hole was closed. She pulled at the dirty cloth gently to test it. It wasn't pretty, but she thought it would hold the weight.

The shirt went back over her head slowly. To her relief the credits stayed in place. How much time had passed? She couldn't leave the credits on the floor, so she bent to pick them up. It would only take a moment and then she would be away.

The foreman walked by the window then, alone. He glanced at the tinted glass with surprise, then alarm. Mira had just enough time to grab the last few credits from the floor and jump against the wall before he burst inside.

His face was blank, and he stood in the doorway for a long moment. His eyes never left Mira's as he walked around his desk and sat. She stared back, resisting the urge to glance in the direction of the drawer.

"I understand your reluctance to be seen in my office," Jin said, his voice cold and formal, "but you will never touch my desk again. Even to darken the window."

Mira's hand trembled at her side. She held it with the other hand and stammered an apology, keeping very still to keep the credits in her hidden pocket from clinking together. *I was supposed to be gone by now.* What was she supposed to do?

"Well?" said the foreman, now impatient. "Why did you need to see me?"

"I..." Mira's mind raced for an excuse. "I wanted to thank you. For the extra credits you gave me. My daughter is doing much better."

"Good, I had wondered. Does she eat enough? I need to keep a balanced payroll, but I may have something extra..." he reached for the drawer.

"No!" she blurted, raising a hand toward him. The credits on her back shifted. "She's fine now, better than fine. You've already done enough, more than I deserve."

He removed his hand from the drawer. Mira barely stifled a sigh. Jin tilted his head and said, "What's her name? Your daughter?"

Why was he asking her daughter's name? Was something wrong? He didn't look like he suspected anything, but Melisao were hard to gauge.

His stare was piercing, so she looked down–and spotted three more credits, on the ground at the edge of his desk. She must have missed them. Her eyes shot back up, but Jin's gaze was unmoved. Had he seen the discs when he entered? Was he delaying her so peacekeepers could arrive? She didn't know if he could alert them without her knowing.

"Ami. My other girl is Kaela." Sweat trickled down her back, pooling at the spot where the pocket rested against her skin. The longer she stood there the more her nerve withered. Was he testing her? If she admitted to her crime he might be lenient. Maybe that was what was happening: the foreman was giving her a chance to confess. She felt like a fool, standing there with a pile of stolen credits on her back. Why did she ever think she could get away with it?

He nodded. "I know how it feels to work a difficult job, to provide for the ones you love." He looked like he wanted to tell her more, but instead he only said, "Angela looks impatient at your station. You may go, if that is all."

She took one cautious step toward the door; the credits on her back made no noise. No peacekeepers jumped out to arrest her. She shuffled out of the office, past the disapproving stare of the secretary, toward her freedom.

Chapter 8

Mira jingled like a broken machine as she ran down the street. She'd stepped on a sharp piece of debris in her carelessness, and left a trail of red smears behind her. Buildings framed either side of the street and faces watched down from doorways and broken windows. They didn't know if she was in need or in trouble, so they remained in their places, unwilling to risk themselves by interfering.

She didn't know if she even *needed* to run, but she didn't want to take the chance. The workers at the factory had watched her leave the foreman's office and walk straight out the door. They probably thought she lost her job, despite not being escorted from the building by peacekeepers. The foreman may not even realize that she, and the food credits, were gone until the next day. And she had plenty of time to gather her girls and get to the Station in time.

But she ran, because it felt safer than walking.

Her feet slowed when she neared her home, almost an hour later. She left the main street and slipped down an alley, stepping over sleeping people who had no shelter of their own. The alley twisted and turned until it finally opened back out on the main street. Mira stopped. With care she tilted her head around the corner until her building came into view. And so did they: the gang of boys sat on the curb outside, lazily tossing rocks at one-another. They'd loitered around her building for the past few days, forcing Mira to scale the rear wall to reach her room. But the pocket of credits was heavy on her back, and she didn't think she could navigate the meager footholds to the fourth floor with bloodied feet.

Instead she turned back into the alley. She found another road surrounded by apartments, running parallel to the main street. It opened onto a side street that bordered her building. She followed the wall until she was at the corner by the entrance. She could hear them now, laughing and taunting the three prostitutes that sat on the steps by the door.

She couldn't slip inside while their attention was on the doorway, so she hugged the wall and waited.

She watched the sand dunes to the south. She imagined she could see one shrink while another grew, the sand shifted by the constant wind. If she squinted she even thought she could see people along the top, tiny black specks from that distance. The longer she watched the more she realized how tired she was. Her eyes were playing tricks on her.

The dying sun drifted through the hazy sky but the boys stayed outside her building. There was a window next to Mira that she considered entering before dismissing the idea. The only people who dared live on the ground floor were those who could defend themselves, and they would likely kill her before asking her intentions. It would be safer trying to climb the wall with bloody feet.

Finally it grew quiet. She peered around the corner. The boys were still there in the street, but they had moved away from the door. They were gathered in a circle, poking and prodding something on the ground. A bug, or an animal. Something distracting. She wondered if it was enough, but her time was growing short.

She mustered what courage she could and rounded the corner. It felt like a death march, walking the twenty feet from the corner to the door. She looked straight ahead, as if that might help. The boys kept their backs turned to her. She watched them at the edge of her vision with a lump in her throat. The prostitutes looked up at her approach, but to Mira's relief didn't care enough to acknowledge her.

She was on the steps, just a few short strides from safety, when one of the boys yelled, "There she is!"

She bolted through the doorway and up the winding stairs. She moaned as she counted, floor two, floor three, until she reached the fourth. She was hobbling down her hallway then, the gashes on her feet even worse than before. There were sounds behind her, urging her faster. She felt like they were just behind, almost within reach of her.

She burst into her room. Her daughters yelled but she didn't care. She slammed the door and fell to the ground, leaning her back against the rotten wood. It had no lock, and her weight would hardly hold the door against their strength, so she put a finger to her lips to silence the girls.

She twisted her head, listening for anything in the hallway, but the only sound was of her own ragged breathing.

Only when she was certain they were safe did she stand and go to the window. The boys were still there in the street, ringing the entranceway, metal clubs held with malicious intent. Standing in front of the door were the three prostitutes, knives at-hand.

"Come now, little boy," one of them called, "Old Sasha will give you a sweet kiss."

The boys threw curses back at the women, but made no move forward. Finally the largest woman said, "Bugger off now, or we'll tell Bruno you've been making trouble down here for days. You think he'd like to hear that?"

That threat succeeded where the others failed, and the boys lowered their weapons. One by one they slinked away. They didn't go far though, stopping just a block away in the direction of the Station. They sat down there, in the middle of the street. One of them looked up to where Mira was. She pulled her head back inside.

"What's wrong, mama?" Kaela finally asked.

Mira gathered the few things that belonged to them and wrapped them in one of the blankets. "We're leaving. We're going to Oasis, just like I promised."

Kaela was unconvinced. "That's just a story you told us, to make us feel safe."

"Everything I've told you about Oasis is true," Mira said. "We're leaving tonight, on a ship that will leave this planet and sail to the stars."

"Don't forget my medicine!" Ami chirped.

For once Mira's smile was not forced. "You won't need it anymore, sweet girl."

She led them out of the room and down the hallway, where a window opened to the alley below. Climbing down was easier than up, but the sight of the ground so far below gave her pause. "We're going to need to climb now," she said. "I'm going to go first with Ami on my back. Then you'll follow after me. Okay Kaela? It will be like a game. You have to copy every step I make."

Kaela was too old to be fooled by such tricks, but she nodded anyways.

Mira stepped over the window and onto the ledge. She waited for Ami to crawl up and put her arms around her neck. Kaela handed her their blanket of belongings, which dangled in front of Mira's chest. With a deep breath she stepped down from the ledge. The building was haphazardly built with clay bricks, and Mira felt around with her foot before finding one that stuck out enough. She lowered herself to it, changing hand-holds along the way. She repeated the process again and again, making her way down the wall. The blood on her feet slowed the descent, but her purchase at every step was secure.

Ami dropped from her neck when they reached the bottom. Kaela was right behind them and landed softly. Ami laughed as if it was a game.

They followed more side streets and alleys to avoid the gang before returning to the main boulevard. They hurried on to the Station, Mira carrying Ami when she had the strength while Kaela ran alongside. The girls still didn't fully grasp what was happening, but they saw their mother smiling and mirrored her hope.

The Station looked lifeless in the daytime, with none of the noise and color it held at night. Two of the guards were sleeping, and the others didn't bother to watch them enter. Through the front door of the main building they went, stepping over sleeping people in the hallway. Ami pointed as they passed the doctor's office, but Mira had eyes only for the large door at the end of the hall. It was a massive square of metal, cold to her touch. In the center was a monster painted in red. It was a long, slithering thing that wrapped around itself, ending in a head that bore two sharp fangs. The girls stared at it with a mixture of curiosity and wonder.

Mira banged on the door. A few bodies in the hallway stirred, but went back to sleep as the echo faded away. A small eye-hole opened from the painted monster's mouth but closed again before she could look up. The door shook as massive bolts unlocked. Finally it swung inward on thick hinges.

Though the rest of the Station slumbered, the core chamber was very much alive. The room was cavernous, taking up most of the building's space. The ceiling let sunlight through so far overhead that Mira couldn't tell if it was made of glass or simply a gaping hole. A bay door occupied the entire wall to the right. It looked like a door made for receiving shipments, and felt out of place in the room.

In one corner people stood around tables, throwing metal dice and yelling at the result. Their demeanor seemed violent; they pushed and shoved one-another after every dice throw, but then laughed and drank yellow liquid from cups.

A raised platform divided the room itself in half. On the lower half a line of people with a scattering of children waited to enter a door to the left. Some of them held sacks of belongings, but most brought nothing for the journey. They wouldn't need anything on Oasis, the neutral space station that orbited between Praetar and Melis. Food and clothing would be provided there, they all knew. Nobody was turned away on Oasis, no matter the color of their eyes.

The raised platform held a chair with a high back.

81

On it sat Bruno, the self-titled Lord of the Station. While most Praetari were scrawny he was huge, with a bloated stomach that pressed tightly against his yellow shirt. His hair was brown and tattered, his skin red and blotchy. A man spoke to him but he didn't seem to listen; he looked around the room with tiny, squinting eyes. Guards with guns surrounded him on the platform, watching the line of dirty people with distrust.

"Yes, yes, you'll be fine," Bruno said. "The freighters have weapons, should the Empire enforce the siege. Your family will get through."

That seemed to placate the man, who returned to his family in line.

Mira approached the platform. She set Ami down and pulled her arms into her shirt, lifting it over her head while taking care not to spill the credits from the hidden pocket. The guards leered at her bare chest, but Mira ignored them. She turned her shirt over and poured the credits onto the platform in a cascade of glass. Every head in the room turned toward the sound. When she put her shirt back on there was still a handful of glass discs inside, but the pile on the platform was more than enough.

"One hundred and fifty credits, at least," she said, a note of pride in her voice. "Three passengers to Oasis."

It was done. All of her work, the credit saving, the frugal meals. All of it was over. They were alive. They made it.

Bruno squinted down at her and laughed, a deep,

sickening sound. "I did not expect you to earn the fare so quickly," he said, "especially after that one grew sick."

There was a hint of question in his voice, but Mira didn't indulge his curiosity. She'd never met him before, but somehow he knew her.

He smiled, a cruel grin that flashed cracked yellow teeth. "Although we accept your payment, the ship is nearly full. Only two of you may come."

"No..." Mira said. No, it didn't make sense. "Look at my girls, they're tiny. Two can share a crate."

"You misunderstand," Bruno said. "There is only *one* crate available, so soon before the launch. You can squeeze into it with the daughter of your choice, but three will not fit."

She stared, uncomprehending. Her mind felt slow and soft. It occurred to her how tired she was.

"Is there no room anywhere? No corner one of them can squeeze?"

"We could bolt the smaller one to the hull outside," he said, "but I don't think she would enjoy the journey."

The guards roared with laughter, and Mira looked around helplessly. Her daughters stared at her, not understanding, but she couldn't look at them.

The passengers in line were still watching. She went to them to plead her case. "Can anyone share a crate with my girl? Her name is Ami, she's so small, you would never even notice her. I just need a small bit of space."

She spotted a man by himself. She grabbed his sleeve and said, "Can't you make room for a tiny girl? She's sick, she needs to *leave*, please. I'll pay you, I have extra credits." The man pulled away from her.

Mira looked around. The passengers ignored her; most wouldn't even look in her direction. They were there for the same reason she was, and wouldn't risk their own families. She might do the same in their position. Her hand trembled. She couldn't turn back to her children.

"The next freighter leaves in three days," Bruno offered.

Three days would be too late. They didn't even have three *hours* before her theft was discovered. She made herself look at her girls. They stared back with hope. Kaela put her arm around her sister, and they both smiled. They're brave, so brave.

Mira took one last look around the room: at the ceiling that showed freedom beyond, at the line of people that ignored her, at the guards with their weapons. And at the slumlord who watched it all with a smile.

"Both of my daughters will go. I'll stay behind."

The line led outside to where rows of empty metal crates sat in the dirt. The passengers were stuffed inside each one, and when it was her daughters' turn Mira blinked away her tears.

"You'll meet us on Oasis?" Kaela's eyes were wide with excitement, ready for the adventure. It was real to her now, not just a story told before bed.

"Of course. I'll be on the next freighter."

"How long will it take?" Ami asked, looking inside the crate.

"Only a few days. The trip will be over before you know it. And then I'll be there, and we'll find a place to live together, and it will be wonderful." She couldn't hold back tears then, and squeezed them both tightly so they wouldn't see. "I love you so much," she murmured into Kaela's hair. "Take care of your sister until I meet you."

They were warm in her arms, smiling brightly when she finally let go. They were going somewhere better than this. They were going to be safe.

The girls stepped inside the crate and crouched together against the wall. If they were scared they didn't show it. Their faces disappeared as one of Bruno's brutes covered the crate with a piece of metal and bolted it down at the corners.

The freighter was an ugly thing, all flat edges and pointed corners. Its only decoration was a coiled green animal on its side, the same one that marked the entrance to the Station. The doors to its storage bay were open like a jaw, and two men lifted the crates and stacked them neatly inside. So orderly was the storage that when they were complete, and the doors closed, Mira wouldn't have been able to wedge her hand inside, let alone her entire person.

She didn't want to leave, but eventually tore her eyes

away.

Back inside the Station core Bruno held a wide metal bowl in his hand, spooning its contents into his mouth. Her credits were gone from the platform. "Is there a place here I can stay, until the next freighter?" she asked.

"You can watch this one leave, but after that you must pay to stay." Bruno didn't bother to stop eating while he spoke, and soup dribbled down his chin.

"There were enough credits leftover, surely," she said.

His smile was cruel. "Not so. Your credits were counted, and there were just enough for two passengers. Unless you think Rief miscounted."

The guard to Bruno's left sneered. "Aye, there were one hundred credits exactly. Not one disc more."

Bruno waved his spoon. "So you see? The matter is decided. You may work for me if you wish to stay, but I fear it will be many months before you earn enough to leave. Count yourself lucky you have a factory job, and two fewer mouths to feed."

Mira stared helplessly. For a moment she almost dared to argue, but the watching guards changed her mind. There was a boredom among them, a restlessness that said they would love nothing more than for her to protest.

Instead she fled, with their laughter chasing her from the room.

She passed through the Station gate, gazing down the long road that led back toward the city. She couldn't go home; the peacekeepers would look for her there, as soon as the theft was discovered. They might even be there now. But she couldn't stay at the Station, not at Bruno's price.

She looked to the south. The sand dunes rose high in the distance, their crests indistinguishable from the hazy sky. How far away were they? No more than an hour walk, she thought. She wondered what was on the other side.

The ground vibrated. She turned back to the Station. The explosion reached her ears, and then a deafening roar, like a million tiny pops all at once. A flare of light appeared above the Station's roof, the metallic glint of the freighter visible above it. She watched it soar into the sky, a flickering fire that shone through the yellow haze of the planet. She imagined Kaela and Ami sitting inside their crate. They wouldn't be afraid, she knew.

She watched until the sound died away, and then until the light disappeared. Only a string of smoke remained. For a long while she watched that too.

Finally she turned back south. She took a deep breath and walked onto the sand.

Tales of a Dying Star

Part III: The Snake

Tales of a Dying Star

Chapter 9

"I'm in the business of selling hope."

Bruno didn't address anyone in particular, but he felt the need to say something as he watched the freighter through the ceiling window. His thick neck ached as it craned back, but he always enjoyed watching the ships soar away on billowing pillars of smoke. Each launch was like a ritualistic sacrifice; an offering to the Melisao blockade and the Emperor far away. He fingered the short knife on his hip. Bruno was not a religious man, but there was something comforting about the ritual.

"Never forget the valuable service we provide," he said. "Without us the people would lose hope, and the planet would shrivel and die."

The guards standing around the table where he ate didn't respond as they too watched the sky. He owed them no explanations. They were his to command, fiercely loyal; they would rip each other to shreds at his word. If they cared at all for the men and women on the doomed freighters they wisely kept it to themselves.

Besides, the passengers knew the danger. If they wanted to continue toiling for the Empire they wouldn't have come to him. There was sweat and blood and death aplenty on their miserable yellow planet, but *hope* was a precious thing indeed, and its only purveyor was Bruno.

Only when the ship was long out of sight did he return his gaze to the meal. A man with his sway didn't suffer the food of a common Praetari. A dozen plates covered the table with every manner of delicacy: fresh bread baked from imported flour, indoor clams swimming in cream, fatty meat from some fowl he couldn't even recognize. But what Bruno savored most was the *gaba broush*, the mushy meal mixed with oil once eaten by the ancient kings of Praetar. The seasonal crop it was made from grew only on the surface of the vast sulfuric ocean covering most of the planet. It was deadly to attempt to swim out and harvest, but the bounty Bruno offered was high. Every year several bushels made their way into his possession.

Only one chair was needed for the feast, and Bruno filled every inch of it.

As was customary he ate the *gaba broush* with his hands, careless of the mess he made. Grease smeared his face and ran down his chin, his yellow shirt long since soiled.

His men watched him out of the corner of their eyes, not daring to stare openly at the table of food. Power was derived in many ways; the Empire's rationing of food kept its grip on the planet strong. Bruno understood that well.

"Loddac," he said around a mouthful of mush, "come join me."

The guard glanced at the others as if he'd heard wrong. Bruno had to gesture at the food before he stepped forward. He didn't hesitate at all then, throwing his gun over his shoulder and shoving handfuls of food into his mouth from whichever plates were closest.

"Thank you, Lord Bruno," he said through half-chewed bread. Such rich food would make him sick later, Bruno knew, but it was only a passing thought. It was the reward that mattered, not whether he could keep it all down.

Kotra and Rief eyed their fellow guard as he feasted with faces dark and scowling. They were competent guards, as cruel and eager to violence as Bruno could hope for, and they'd done nothing to deserve exclusion. But a reward wasn't a reward if it was given to everyone, and Loddac was the first name that popped into his head.

There were other ways to motivate a man, as well. Some of Bruno's most loyal guards were those he'd treated unfairly. The child spurned by its mother is the one most eager for her approval.

His stomach was overfull, so he turned his chair away

from the table to face the open room. It was mostly empty now that the freighter was gone, but a few men gambled at the table in the corner and others drank yellow liquid at the bar.

He turned his gaze to the woman bent prostrate in front of his platform. She was a boney thing, with hardly enough flesh to be called a woman. The only reason he knew her sex at all was because she'd come to him before. "Get up."

She stood shakily, whether from stiffness at waiting so long, or from hunger, or for another reason. Her eyes immediately looked to the polished wooden box on a pedestal to Bruno's left, not to the table of food. Bruno knew the reason for her appearance. He looked down on her with disinterest, letting the silence grow while she fidgeted.

"Lord Bruno," she finally said, but he pointedly interrupted her.

"What is it that you want, Tavia?"

She flinched at his voice. She refusing to meet his gaze, her eyes still fixed on the box. "I came only to thank you, Lord Bruno. I know you are extremely busy–"

"I cannot abide liars. Do you come into the Station, my *home*, and lie outright? What would my men think if they heard this in my presence?"

His guards laughed obediently. Even Loddac, who spit bits of food across the table.

"Tell me why you are here, in truth, or you only

94

presume to waste my time."

With every word she seemed to hunch into herself, until she was nearly crouching. "I came for another bit of *plourine*. I need it." She let it all out in a rush, unable hold back her tears any longer.

Bruno watched her sob, soft gasps that were hardly more than a whisper. She didn't seem to have the energy to cry more emphatically. "You have to work before I can give you more. I have *rules*, Tavia."

"I can't," she said, shaking now. "I mean, I can't do it first. I need the plourine first, Lord Bruno. Please. You don't know how it feels."

Bruno smiled as she cried. He knew she would be useless until she had more of the drug, but it was better this way, with people watching. "I am feeling merciful," he said.

He nodded to Rief, who walked to the pedestal and opened the box on its hinge. Green light glowed from within. Every eye in the room watched as he removed a single round tablet with two fingers. Bruno shuddered in spite of himself. Whatever ecstasy it may offer, it wasn't worth the eventual side effects.

Tavia trembled, looking like she wanted to dash onto the raised platform but somehow held her place. Rief walked to her. She opened her mouth to receive the glowing drug. He delicately placed it inside and wiped his hand on his jacket. As if that would help.

Bruno watched to make sure she swallowed the pill.

Plourine was his alone. He took every precaution to ensure it wasn't smuggled out of the Station.

The next part he watched eagerly. Tavia clenched her eyes shut until tears ran down her face. She trembled again, this time with pleasure, and though no noise came out her mouth opened as if to moan. Her feet moved a tiny step forward and she fell to her knees. Finally she opened her eyes and looked around the room as if seeing it all for the first time.

"Visit Leo before you begin work," he said in dismissal, his attention already elsewhere. The Station's scrap engineer, Dok, had entered during Tavia's ordeal and now waited at the edge of the room. Bruno waved him over while Tavia left in a daze.

Dok didn't bow or acknowledge the Lord of the Station in any manner, which would have been a severe insult from anyone else. That was just the way it was with the cloud-headed engineer. He was a fidgeting man, compulsively adjusting the many pieces of metal and gearwork strewn about his long coat while he stood there. He'd explained to Bruno each contraption's purpose, but had bored him near to death with every detail. Dok's brain was as gifted as any on Praetar, but lacked normal social interaction. His autistic leanings were accepted though; the men of the Station found him endearing.

He fidgeted more than usual, which made Bruno frown. As far as emotions, that was the closest thing to fear the engineer possessed. "Tell me, Dok," he said.

"Delivery didn't come." He looked around the

platform, as if one of the guards had the answer. "No delivery, no parts. No parts, no rowbits."

Bruno kept his face a mask, but underneath he seethed. "Leave us," he said to the men gambling in the corner. They were surprised at being addressed, but quickly fled the room with their cups of metal dice. Only when they were gone, and the door was closed, did Bruno speak again.

"Has he sent a message, at least?"

"No messages, no words, no letters," Dok said, twisting a metal gear fastened around his neck. "If delivery is late, Dok is late. And if Dok is late, Bruno is *angry.*"

"I'm not angry," he said, waving a hand. *At least not with you.* Fear was a poor motivator for a man like Dok.

He glanced at the wall to his left. A single bay door filled the wall, huge and imposing. Behind it lay the warehouse where Dok's products were stored. "How many have you completed?"

"Seventy-two. Seventy-two completed." The fingers on his left hand began counting, though Dok didn't seem to notice.

"It's fine," Bruno said. "You've done fine, Dok. Relax for a bit. There's food here, if you're hungry."

He turned to the table, still counting with his left hand. He picked a small piece of bread without looking and wandered back through the smaller door to the engineering room.

Rief and Kotra looked at the table of food longingly, but Bruno didn't notice. His head was beginning to throb. "He will not be pleased," he muttered, massaging his eyes with two thick fingers. Seventy-two was behind schedule, and Bruno had made too many assurances already. *Maybe he won't come tonight.*

But he knew that was a feeble wish. As night fell the Station pumped music and swelled with gamblers and addicts and whores. Tavia was among the latter, still aloof in her radioactive high, but Bruno had eyes only for the front door. Customers came and went, danced in the throng on the floor and retired with women to private rooms. Men drank, and collapsed, and then drank some more. All the while Bruno tapped his fingers and waited.

It was well into the night when he finally appeared in the doorway. Akonai was a tall man with short-cropped white hair, though he couldn't have seen more than forty years. His tan pants and coat were orderly, fitting his slender frame well. He wasn't at all what you would expect from one of the sand dwellers, who lived in the Praetari desert and rarely visited the city.

He glided through the room, the people on the floor parting before him. Loddac rushed to fetch another chair from an adjacent room, placing it next to Bruno on the platform. Akonai climbed the steps and lowered himself into the chair. He met Bruno's eyes. Bruno shot a look at Loddac and waited until the guard had moved a few steps away before speaking.

"Welcome to the Station," he said above the booming

music. "Everything we have is yours, of course."

"I would like an update, please." His voice was cold and formal, every syllable crisp.

Bruno hesitated before answering. he considered distracting the man with women or *plourine*, but Akonai entertained few vices. The Lord of the Station spread his hands wide and smiled. "Unfortunately we've had some setbacks. One of our suppliers failed to make his last two deliveries."

"How many are ready?"

"Ninety-five," he said. He pulled a rag from his pocket and dabbed at the sweat on his face. The *gaba broush* roiled in his stomach. "Ninety-five completed. So you see, we are only *slightly* behind. My men will work twice as hard, I can assure you."

Akonai's eyes were piercing. "Very well," he said, not acknowledging the lie, "so long as you meet the required date."

Bruno sighed. He began to offer the man refreshments, but Akonai was already out of his chair and leaving the platform. He watched him disappear into the front hallway. For a long while Bruno stared at the door as if he might suddenly reappear.

"Rief," he finally called. The guard stepped to his side. "Tomorrow's plans have changed. I will need to visit the factory myself."

Chapter 10

Saria was an angry ball of red on the horizon when the procession left the Station. Bruno brought half of his hired men whenever he left his little fortress, though they couldn't risk carrying guns in the open. Three of them led the way with various metal clubs at hand. Next came two brutes carrying a rough wooden chest by the handles, their own blunted weapons tucked into ragged cloth belts.

Behind them rode Bruno, the only man not burdened with walking. The little electric cart wasn't fast, but it bore his weight dutifully, its only protest a soft clinking of the motor and gears. One wheel was slightly smaller than the other three, so every few moments it rocked back and forth.

Dok shuffled along behind the cart, muttering to

himself and counting on his fingers. He was anxious at leaving his little electronic cave, but Bruno didn't trust his mechanical ride enough to leave the engineer behind. If he must suffer the errands of the day, so must Dok. He had little to do back at the Station anyway until they began receiving factory shipments.

A pair of guards flanked the electronic cart, and six more rounded out the rear. It occurred to him that it was an overzealous party, but Bruno didn't want to take any chances. The desert people grew bolder, even raiding in the daylight. Whatever their motives, he didn't want to leave himself vulnerable. Akonai was civilized, but he couldn't be sure about the other desert dwellers.

It didn't hurt to make a show of force occasionally, either.

Praetar was a long city that ran along the thin strip of land between the sulphur oceans and the deserts. There was one long boulevard that was the backbone, with the Station near one end and the greater Empire structures at the other. The planet had scarcely been rebuilt after the invasion, and most buildings had gaping holes and broken windows still unrepaired. There was no intact glass whatsoever. Some buildings missed whole floors entirely, while others were nothing more than piles of rubble.

From alleyways and windows, roofs and doorways, people watched the Lord of the Station proceed. It was rare that he ventured from his territory. Many had likely only heard stories of him. "Unpleasant stories," Bruno muttered, looking down an alley to his left. The group of children there disappeared deeper into the alley, as though falling under his gaze would bring some unknown punishment.

He smiled to himself. It was a reaction he was used to, had worked to foster. Even as a boy he knew the importance of fear. He'd scrounged around with other bored children, looting and robbing where the Empire didn't care to police. A man could protect his store against one boy, but not against five, and every window not destroyed when the Empire came was broken by Bruno's gang.

But it wasn't enough that the other boys followed him. There was ambition in youth, a desire to push above one's place. That was fine in a leader like Bruno. Leaders *needed* ambition, or they were destined to rule a small gang hiding from the Empire for their whole life.

But ambition was poison in a follower. A man needed to know his place, and sometimes that was a difficult lesson to learn.

Bruno was larger than the others, both in size and strength. Killing the boy was easy, a scrawny little rat named Donno. He needed only knock him down and get on top and smash his head into the ground until the yellow dirt stained black. Donno had done nothing wrong, but it didn't matter. The others all stood around and watched, and when Bruno walked away they followed.

The cart rocked on its misshapen wheel, jolting him

out of his memories.

Bruno eyed the guard to the left of the cart. Rief was one of the taller men, with wide shoulders and thighs as strong as steel. Bruno looked down at his own heft splayed across the cart. He doubted he could kill one of his own men now. "Maybe if I fell on him and smothered him with my gut," he announced with a chuckle.

Rief glanced over but said nothing.

Power deriving from physical intimidation became inadequate eventually. A strong arm may break a man's bone, but only one at a time. Better to possess a dozen strong arms, never having to lift a finger himself.

A strong arm couldn't do everything though, he realized as his cart clinked down the road. Bruno's men knew little more than violence, and their tasks that day required finesse, intelligence. They were good for what they were, but sometimes there was no substitute for Bruno himself.

The little parade came to a stop outside the market where common Praetari received their food. Bruno pressed a button and the cart hissed to a stop. The men carrying the chest sighed with relief, releasing it to the ground with a clatter that drew every eye on the now busy street. He would need to scold them for that later.

His finely-polished boots crunched in the dirt as he walked inside the market. Two guards flanked him. There was a long line waiting for food–there always was–but Bruno need not suffer through it. He strode to the front counter with his chin held high. The people in line looked first with annoyance, then with fear, as they realized who he was. None dared to speak against him, and all conversations ceased.

The Station held more food than most of Praetar combined, but there was something to be said for keeping up appearances. With gusto Bruno greeted the Melisao peacekeepers handing out food as if they were all long-lost brothers. He thanked them for their service and praised the Emperor's wisdom. He selected a loaf of bread, slid a single credit across the counter, and boasted of its flavor as he chewed. And while all eyes were on him, his guard slipped a package to one of the peacekeepers who judged its weight and nodded.

With that done Bruno said his goodbyes and turned to leave. He tossed the loaf of bread back and forth between his hands. The line of Praetari eyed it eagerly. Once in the doorway he tossed it over his shoulder. The sound of people scrambling for the bread made him smile.

He followed his guards around the side of the building to a narrow alleyway. The men carrying his chest fell in behind. The alley stretched a long way, showing that the market was far larger than the part facing the street. Above them glassless windows led to the building's second floor, the sound of machinery and labor drifting into the alley. Bruno licked his lips and tried not to think of the bite of bread he swallowed, or from where it had come.

Bruno's breath was labored by the time the alley opened into a square courtyard. Three tall doors lined the rear of the market building where supplies could be delivered from the narrow road that led in the opposite direction. Only one door was open now, and at the edge of darkness stood a single man.

He wore a crisp black uniform and held his hands behind his back, which pulled the coat tight across his flat chest. His head was cleanly shaven. His nose was the size of an oyster, with piercing blue eyes behind it that watched intently. He smiled as they approached. "Hello, Bruno."

"How fares the Empire, Davon?"

"The exodus grows near. How much do you bring today?"

Bruno wanted to ask more, but held his tongue. Davon was not generous with his information, and although they were equals in their arrangement, Bruno had no illusions as to who was more powerful. "Seven thousand, six hundred."

The brutes approached the doorway and dropped the chest, more carefully than before. Melisao peacekeepers in white uniforms came forward from the blackness behind Davon and lifted the chest before disappearing again.

They stood there facing one another, Bruno and the officer, while the credits were counted. Finally a voice of affirmation came from inside.

Davon nodded. "Very well. Your account will be

credited presently." Typically that was the end of their transaction, but the Melisao officer lingered. "Do you still launch ships full of refugees, Bruno?"

Bruno's breath caught in his throat. It was a topic they rarely discussed. "Aye, we do. As requested."

"How often?"

"Every few days," Bruno said. "More than that, when Dok has the parts." It was a nonsense question. The roaring launches were hardly secret and could be seen from anywhere in the city.

Davon considered that. "We want them to become more frequent. A launch every day is ideal."

"That's a lot of work," Bruno said, spreading his hands, "and I've only got the one engineer. My price will go up."

Davon shrugged. "Begin daily launches first. Prove to me that you are still useful, and then you will be paid." With that he turned and disappeared inside, the door closing with a clang.

They retreated back down the alley. A growing unease filled Bruno, as whenever he made the exchange. Not because of any intimidation or fear, but because he was clueless to Davon's motivations. None of it made sense. Why launch ships into orbit to crumple against the blockade? And an officer of the Empire had no use for the planet's food credits. So why would he purchase the small, glass discs from Bruno?

Davon was the one who approached him with the

offer, a year prior. Food credits for Melisao credits, exchanged once a week. The Empire had no physical money, instead using an electronic ledger system to transfer wealth among its populace. The ledger was public and pseudonymous; everyone could see the balance of any other account but had no idea to whom each account belonged. That made it simple for the Empire to track all transactions, while still allowing a modicum of anonymity for its citizens.

Bruno was using the account of a dead peacekeeper, or so Davon claimed. There was an entire economy on Praetar based around food credits, but control of a Melisao account gave him a new tier of power. Peacekeepers could now be bribed, more exotic goods acquired. Such as electroid parts.

Davon knew which account was Bruno's, however, so he had to know it was used for such activity. But he didn't seem to care. Why allow him to continue using it, why give it to him in the first place, and why exchange useless food credits for legitimate money?

He shook his head. The questions had plagued him ever since the arrangement began, and he still had no answers that day. All he knew was that it afforded him more power. That the power came at Davon's behest, and could cease on his whim, was a worry for another time.

The electric cart creaked as he resumed his seat, his guards returning to their posts on either side. That should have been the end of the day, but Bruno had more unpleasant business to deal with. Instead of

107

returning to the Station they continued on, deeper into the city.

The buildings that flanked the road grew larger the farther east they went, more industrial than residential. Black smoke rose from brick stacks above the factories, and the hum of machinery created a din in the background. It was close to midday so the streets were deserted. Bruno allowed the cart to rock him to sleep.

It felt like his eyes had barely shut when a voice woke him.

"Sinners!" screamed the man from the side of the road. He wore a brown robe that had probably once been white, with long sleeves that hung low as he pointed. "You ignore the noon-day prayer!"

The Prophet was a common sight. He wandered the city preaching the worship of Saria, condemning those who didn't pray when she was brightest in the sky. The Praetari mostly ignored him. The peacekeepers just laughed. He was harmless, an aged relic of the sun-worshiping religion wiped-out when the Empire came.

He didn't mind being called a sinner. The Prophet yelled the insult at anyone and everyone. But Bruno was dusty from the ride and unhappy at being woken. He gestured and Loddac left the group. Bruno turned away and yawned. The Prophet cried out but then was silenced. A few moments later Loddac returned to them, blood dripping from his club.

Their destination was a wide factory that stretched an entire block along the boulevard. It had no windows; its entrance was plain double doors. Once again Bruno climbed from his cart, gesturing at Rief to join him. He considered Loddac a moment before waving him along too. Blood on the guard's club would add emphasis to Bruno's words.

It took several blinks to adjust before he could see in the factory's dim light. One long conveyor belt snaked its way through the room, with women spaced along the belt every twenty feet assembling parts. His presence was an aberration, and every worker stared with open mouths.

He turned left and walked along the wall, conscious of their eyes. It made him smile. If they were surprised by his visit Jin would be too.

The secretary rose from her desk outside the office when he approached. She looked Bruno up and down, unsure of what to say. He'd never visited the factory before but she surely knew who he was. She made some protesting noises but he ignored them. Rief opened the office door and Bruno strode inside.

The man behind the desk was not Jin.

He had the blue eyes of a Melisao, but that was the only similarity. Where Jin had been stocky this man was slim. His short, thin hair was the color of Praetari mud, and his eyes were too close together. "Who are you?" the man said.

They were the exact words Bruno had opened his mouth to say. "Where's Jin?" he asked instead.

The man looked past Bruno to the doorway, where

the secretary's head appeared. Rief put his arm around her shoulder and led her away, slamming the door behind him.

"Jin was arrested yesterday," the man said, now flushed. "I'm Lenir, the new foreman."

Bruno's heart jumped into his throat. Was Jin removed for dealing with him? If his work was discovered peacekeepers should have already stormed the Station. They could be there right now, waiting for him to return.

He regarded Lenir carefully. "Why was he removed?"

"He was stealing food credits. Hundreds of them, apparently. As if the Governor wouldn't find out."

Bruno felt relieved, but only for a moment. It had taken a long time to dig his claws into Jin, but once he had, the deliveries came every week, never late. And here was Lenir, staring at him cluelessly. Losing Jin was a blow to his plans indeed.

Something on Bruno's face must have scared the man. His hand reached out to push a button on the desk. The motion caused Loddac to raise his club, scaring Lenir back against the wall. The office window suddenly shifted, tinting to conceal their meeting. The guard lowered his weapon, though Lenir was still pressed against the wall. Bruno smiled. This may go easier than he expected.

"My name is Bruno. I'm a businessman." The office held only one chair, so Bruno stepped closer to the desk. "Jin and I had an arrangement, one I would like to extend to you. You are a lucky man, Lenir."

From his pocket Bruno pulled a small square device. It was more advanced than anything a Praetari ought to own, with a computer screen on the front and some electronics encased behind. There were two numbers visible on the screen: a sixteen-digit account number, and then the balance below. Buttons on the side allowed him to scroll through a list of transactions. Davon's deposit was already listed, he saw.

"What is your Melisao account number?" he asked Lenir.

The foreman hesitated, taking another long look at Loddac before rattling off sixteen numbers and letters. Bruno held down a button while he spoke; the device listened. When he was done a new account displayed on the screen.

Bruno gave an exaggerated laugh. "You are not a rich man, foreman Lenir. But that will change today." He tapped a few commands into the device. "Check your balance now."

Lenir stared at them with wide eyes. He was confused at the conversation, or at Bruno's laughter, or at a Praetari owning a Melisao account at all. He turned to his own screen and moved a few fingers, and then gaped at what he saw.

"Consider that a deposit," Bruno said, replacing his smile with a frown. "Ten fully constructed electroids. Twenty additional power batteries. Twenty separate memory cores, unprogrammed. That is all I require of you."

Lenir sputtered. "How am I supposed to provide those? The Governor sends inspectors every few days to check the factory. They'll know if anything is missing."

"Counterfeit your inventory numbers," Bruno said, "or scrounge from the electroids assembled. Jin had help from some of the workers, I recall. It is your problem to figure out, not mine."

Lenir opened his mouth to speak, but then closed it and gave a nod. Too quickly.

"I know what you are thinking, foreman Lenir," Bruno said. "You will call the peacekeepers as soon as I leave, to tell them of my visit. I can assure you that would be unwise. If I am arrested my account will be discovered, and my transactions examined. And they will see a transaction to your account."

"I've done nothing illegal for you."

"You think they will believe that? You received a sizeable deposit from the Lord of the Station, for nothing in exchange?" He looked to Loddac. "This one's a bigger fool than Jin."

They both laughed. Lenir's eyes grew wide; Bruno knew he had him. "We require those parts delivered once a week. I will send you the location and time."

They left the factory and returned to the cart, and turned it back the way they came. They passed the Prophet moaning on the ground, but otherwise there was nothing to keep Bruno from sleeping soundly all the way back to the Station.

Chapter 11

"I don't care about the details, Dok," Bruno said. "Just tell me when the damn thing will be ready."

Bruno wiped grime from his forehead with a rag, but all it did was smear. The courtyard was enclosed on three sides by various Station rooms, but wind still kicked up dirt and swirled it around the area. Behind him was the door back to the main chamber. To his right was an entranceway to Dok's workshop.

But what occupied their attention, and most of the courtyard, was the freighter. Square-shaped and long, it was similar to most of the others they launched, but with a coiled red snake painted on the side. Their dusty planet had no lack of ships. The Empire was in too much of a hurry to maintain the freighters that carried cargo and supplies from the planet, and it was easier to simply build more in their factories than repair those that broke down. Scrap heaps were dug and fenced-in, but Davon permitted him to enter and take what he needed.

Dok and his crew worked on the ships once they arrived. It usually took little effort to get them launch-ready; they didn't need to fly far. But this particular ship was giving the engineer trouble. The two blocky engines extended away from the hull at the rear of the ship, and Dok had spent three days tinkering inside one. Each day the problems became more complex, his explanations more detailed. Bruno was growing impatient. The Station had many sources of income, but sending desperate civilians into space was the largest.

Dok tapped his foot into the ground, counting. "One day," he finally said. "One day."

Bruno eyed the fidgety man and frowned. One day seemed unlikely, and for a moment he considered arguing, but then he dismissed the thought. Dok was eccentric, but he doubted the man could lie, or even exaggerate. If he said it would be ready tomorrow then it was simply the truth.

"Need more weapons," Dok blurted out. "Still no weapons."

"The ships don't need weapons, Dok."

"But you told the woman. I heard you tell her, the woman with the yellow hair, I *heard*. You said–"

"Damnit Dok," he said, grinding his teeth, "there are no weapons. There will be no weapons!"

115

The little man cringed away from him, and he felt a tinge of guilt. "Dok, what I say to you is not what I say to others. You just listen to what I tell *you*, okay Dok?"

He grunted and continued counting on his fingers, but he nodded.

Bruno spun around to return inside, but Kotra waved at him from the workshop door. "Uhh, Lord Bruno," he said, "there's something here you'll want to see. Err, hear." One of Dok's workers stood next to him, looking uncomfortable.

The workshop was dimly lit. It was one large square with workbenches against each wall. Wires and pieces of metal spread over every surface. It all looked haphazard, though he knew it was orderly to Dok. The only wall not occupied by a workbench was a gap to the right, where a door led to the warehouse, the same one with the huge bay door to Bruno's main chamber. He looked away from it after only a quick glance.

The worker led them to a bench on the left, where boxy electronics were stacked from the table to the ceiling. They looked like they would topple over at the slightest touch, but the worker twisted a knob and pressed a button. A buzz pierced the air and Bruno realized one of them was a speaker.

The speaker crackled, and then a voice drifted through the static. "–hear me? Can you hear me?"

The worker pressed a button and leaned forward. "We hear you, two-forty. Repeat your status, please."

Two-forty was the freighter launched last week. Bruno shot Kotra an alarmed look, but before he could say anything the speaker crackled back to life.

"We were halfway through our acceleration to Oasis when we ran out of fuel. Must have been a leak, or a faulty sensor, or something. I don't know. We're drifting now. Could use some help, the next time you launch."

The worker reached forward to respond, but Bruno grabbed his hand. "Where is the ship now?"

A clockwork map of the system was built into the wall a short distance away. Saria was a stationary ball of red, but its three planets were set into grooves, moved by unseen machinery. Other unnatural objects followed their own grooves: the Ancillary, circling close to the star in retrograde to harvesting its power; various military installations orbiting at strategic distances.

And Oasis, the neutral space station that orbited between Praetar and Melis. Its orbit was faster than either planet, but just then it was close to Praetar.

The worker took a grease pencil and drew an arc away from the yellow planet. "This is their trajectory if they continued accelerating as planned. Here is where they are now. I'll need some time to calculate their drifting route, but by then they'll be out of communication range."

Bruno looked behind him to make sure they were still alone. He didn't want Dok to hear anything. "Let them drift. Tell them we're sending another ship today to help them refuel."

The worker shifted, looking from the radio to Kotra and then back to him. "I don't know what Dok has told you, Lord Bruno, but the next freighter won't be ready today."

"Just send the message." The worker continued to look uncomfortable, but Bruno's stare set him to work. Bruno waited for him to begin speaking into the microphone before leaving the workshop.

Outside Dok tinkered with the freighter's engine, out of earshot. Kotra whispered, "Has the blockade been lifted?"

It was the same question on Bruno's mind. "It must have been. How else would the ship get through?"

"Maybe they missed it."

"The Melisao don't miss things," Bruno said. "If a ship got through the blockade it was because they allowed it to."

"We could leave," Kotra said. The hardened man seemed hopeful, almost child-like then. He ran a hand through his rough hair. "If they're letting ships through we could leave, couldn't we?"

"I'm not a rat, and I won't flee like one," Bruno said. He frowned at his guard. "Is that what you want? To be a slave for the Empire in some faraway system, instead of a free man here?"

"Of course not, Bruno. I just thought you might–"

"You actually believe them?" he said, his anger boiling up. "Saria's burned for billions of years, why should it stop now? It's all an excuse for the Empire, believe me. I'm a king here. The Empire allows me to gather power, and I'll continue doing it until they storm through the doors and kill me on my throne."

Kotra dipped his head. "You're right. I'm sorry, Lord Bruno."

Dok looked up from his engine. Bruno realized he'd been shouting. He lowered his voice and said, "Get rid of the worker inside. Within the hour. Tell him you're taking him into town or something, and do the deed there."

"Do you care if the body's found?"

"No. Just don't let anyone see you."

Kotra smiled and returned to the workshop.

Hopefully Dok doesn't have a fit, he thought. The engineer didn't like new workers. But it had to be done. This one would have asked more questions and started checking fuel levels on outgoing freighters. Dok would eventually find out.

It occurred to him that the tanks would need to be filled more. It meant less profit, but he couldn't have ships communicating back that they were stranded in open space. If word spread business would shrivel, and Davon wouldn't be pleased. No, the freighters would need to be given enough fuel to reach Oasis. He would need to tell Rief, the only one entrusted with fueling the ships.

He wandered over to where Dok worked. The engine's

side panel was removed and the engineer was bent with his upper half inside. Bruno banged a meaty fist on the metal, and Dok jumped out of the engine.

"Have you made progress with Akonai's project?"

Dok's mouth hung open, and his eyes darted around. "Akonai, Akonai's project?"

Bruno forced some patience into his voice. "Yes. The project for Akonai. How many more are built?"

"I don't. I don't *understand*. No shipment this morning, no progress. No new parts, no new rowbits."

"The shipment didn't come?"

"No, Bruno." He cowered back against the engine, his eyes wide. "I'm sorry, sorry. I don't know why. They don't tell me why. I can't..."

Bruno left him stammering apologies and returned inside.

Rief stood on the raised platform watching some gamblers throw dice in the corner. He jerked back to attention, facing forward, when Bruno entered. "The factory shipment," Bruno barked, "did it not arrive?"

"It did not, Lord Bruno."

"Why in the stars wasn't I notified?"

"You were with the girls," Rief said. "You didn't want to be disturbed."

He said it plainly, but it annoyed Bruno all the same. His men should be more fearful when he raised his voice, like Dok. His shift ended soon, but Bruno told him, "Take two men and go to the factory. Bring the foreman here so I may speak with him."

Rief glanced at the dicing table, and for the briefest of moments opened his mouth, but then thought better of it. He grunted and bowed before leaving the chamber, his boots echoing down the front hallway.

Gamblers came and went, whores began their work, and Bruno tapped his fingers on his throne. Food was brought from the kitchen, but he was too buried in thought to eat. The freighter shouldn't have breached the blockade. It was the first, out of dozens launched. The purpose of the blockade was to keep the Praetari laboring while the Empire prepared to leave the system. If the blockade was lifted, did that mean the Empire would soon evacuate Praetar? Was that why Lenir had not made his delivery–because production was tapering off? He would need to ask one of the girls at the factory. Perhaps the woman who sent her children on the last freighter. "She seemed desperate enough," he announced, though nobody dared look up at him.

Davon's request was queer too. It couldn't be a coincidence, him demanding more launches after a freighter escaped safely. Bruno felt helplessly uninformed. He wondered how much Davon would tell him, if he forced the issue.

The sky overhead turned yellow, then grey, then black before Rief returned. Two guards followed behind him, flanking Lenir. The foreman's clothes were dusted with yellow and torn at the collar. Rief grabbed him by the sleeve and threw him to the ground in front of the platform. The customers all shifted to one side of the room before continuing their activity.

Lenir opened his mouth to speak, but Bruno cut him off. "Your shipment did not arrive this morning."

"I cannot do what you ask," he said, still on his knees. "It is not possible. The factory docks are watched throughout the day."

Bruno clenched his jaw until his ears hurt. The foreman wasn't afraid, just confused. At least the previous man, Jin, had the decency to look afraid. "I can assure you it is possible. My men gave you instructions–what more do you need?"

"Your instructions are *wrong*. The docks are not clear at that time. They've doubled the number of peacekeepers, because of my predecessor's theft."

The guards looked to their master. Even some of the Station's patrons stole glances at the platform. Nobody spoke to Bruno that way.

He nodded to Rief, who pulled back his boot and planted a blow on Lenir's head. He fell forward on his chest and groaned, but screamed in earnest when more blows pummeled his ribs. The crowd cringed away. Rief was out of breath when Bruno finally commanded him to stop, but continued to snarl down at the unmoving foreman.

"I don't care what difficulties you encounter. That is

your responsibility. Find a way. Bribe them, if you must."

Lenir possessed enough strength to raise his head. "Bribe them? They are peacekeepers of the Empire!"

I've had enough of this, he thought. "You've already been paid, Melisao. Every moment you delay, your theft becomes more severe." He nodded to one of his guards. "Loddac tells me your family came to Praetar with you. You have a child, a girl of seven?"

Loddac grinned yellow teeth. "That he does, Lord Bruno. Sweet little thing, still pudgy. I bet she's warm."

The wounded man's eyes opened wide.

"So you see?" Bruno said. "Your decision is an easy one! Make your delivery by dusk tomorrow, or we will unburden you further."

Lenir tried to climb to his feet, but slipped and fell back on his face. Eventually two guards stopped laughing long enough to grab him by the shoulders and drag him from the room. The music returned to its normal, booming volume.

Bruno swung his attention to the table, his appetite returning. He picked at a few oysters, slurping them down. He liked a man with a family. A solitary man could take any manner of beating, broken ribs and torn fingernails and needles jabbed into his eyes, and remain fearless. But a man with a family had one purpose, one single reason for living. Only a father could experience true loss, so only a father could experience true fear.

It was pointless to hurt a man's family, though. They

were his primary motivation. Remove his wife, or his children, and you removed his desire for life. And then what leverage would you have over him? Grief was unpredictable, and Bruno was not in the business of taking chances.

No, it was the *threat* that was ideal. Give the man a taste of violence and his mind will imagine something far worse than anything Bruno could do. And Lenir had a long walk back to the city to think.

Still, something was unsettling about the man. He never had this much trouble with Jin, who supplied them with the parts without protest. But Lenir worried him. Bruno was not convinced the shipment would come, and even if it did the foreman would need to be prodded again and again. He seemed like that type of Melisao. Bruno glanced to his left, to the massive bay door that covered most of the wall. They were already too far behind schedule. Akonai was not an understanding customer.

As if the thought conjured him, the desert dweller appeared in the doorway. He looked out over the occupants, the dancers and gamblers and whores, with disgust. He met Bruno's gaze and held it as he strode across the room. The crowd slid away from him, leaving a circle-shaped clearing that drifted toward the front.

One of the guards rushed to fetch a second chair, but Akonai stopped in front of the platform. Everything about him was exactly in its place: his hair was neatly combed and parted, boots shiny and unsmudged. He was foreign in the writhing disarray of the Station. He seemed foreign to the entire planet.

Bruno wiped away sweat from his forehead. "I hadn't expected you, Akonai. It's good to see you, of course, but..."

"I have come for another status update," he said. His face gave no hint of emotion. "I have reason to believe you will not meet the date we agreed upon."

Bruno forced a nervous laugh. "That's absurd. We've had some delays–there always are with such a large request–but they have been minor. What reasons do you have to doubt?"

"I have sources." He looked around the room, his eyes stopping on the bay door. "Our doubts would be eased if I could inspect the product."

"You know that's not possible," Bruno said. "The fabrication process uses unsavory chemicals. My engineers don't mind breathing them, but we don't want to put you at risk."

Akonai tilted his head and watched him, considering his words. He looked like he was inspecting a machine that wasn't broken yet, but was making a strange noise. Sweat stung Bruno's eyes but he forced himself to keep his hands still and match the man's gaze. Why didn't the desert dweller sweat? His clothes were thicker than Bruno's.

Finally Akonai nodded, as if a great decision was made. "No, we don't want that." And with that he left as suddenly as he had come.

When he was out of sight Bruno turned to Loddac and said, "Why wasn't I warned? Are the guards at the gate asleep? Go check. I want any man who isn't alert to be thrashed."

Bruno slumped back into his chair and closed his eyes. If he couldn't make his shipment to Akonai on time he would have the desert people as enemies. If they didn't launch more freighters then Davon would stop tolerating him. He was spread too thin. He felt his power slipping away, like sand through his fingers. Something needed to be done. Something to emphasize that he was in control.

Loddac returned and claimed none of the guards were sleeping, and that they never saw Akonai enter or leave. Bruno didn't believe it, but waved it away. "I need Kari. Find her."

"For Lenir?"

"Maybe."

Loddac smiled, knowing that he may get the foreman's pudgy daughter after all.

Kari was usually somewhere around the Station, and it didn't take Loddac long to return with her. She was the shortest woman in the room, but with round hips and a tiny waist that would have sold well if her head weren't shaved bald. She wasn't one of Bruno's whores–he wouldn't dare suggest it, not even jokingly. Kari was an assassin.

Her thumbs rested behind her belt, and her brown coat swished around her knees as she walked. Where the Station's customers had parted for Akonai, they practically leapt out of Kari's way.

She took the chair that was fetched for Akonai, slouching into it with an arm over the back. She looked around the room with green eyes, bored, as if trying to decide if she would rather be gambling or drinking. For all the sweat on Bruno's face his mouth was dry as dust. He drank deeply from a cup of yellow liquid on the table. "Care for anything, Kari? Stingwater, food, *plourine*..."

She took the cup from his hand and emptied it in one swallow. Her voice was rough like sand, at odds with her petite frame. "Tell me what you need Bruno. There is a boy I must find and do terrible things to."

That could have meant a target, or one of Bruno's prostitutes. He wasn't sure. "A man named Lenir may need to die."

"He is a Melisao." It was a statement, not a question.

"Yes, the foreman of a factory."

"A Melisao death requires a Melisao price."

"Of course," he said, waving a hand. "Whatever you need is yours."

She was silent, and for a moment Bruno thought she would refuse. She rarely took jobs against blue-eyed targets. Finally she nodded.

He told her everything he knew about Lenir: his age,

127

physical description, the factory he oversaw. Loddac gave her the location of his home. Kari didn't write anything down. She simply listened, nodded, and remembered. She had a flawless memory, especially for every favor she'd done for Bruno. "This is the fifth job this month," she said, looking at the table of food.

"I wouldn't need you if everyone obeyed me."

She examined an oyster between her fingers before tossing it back onto the table. "How soon?"

"Not immediately. Perhaps a day. I will know for certain tomorrow night."

A knife was suddenly in Kari's hand, and she speared a roasted leg of meat. With deft skill she cut away everything from the bone, letting the fatty meat fall back to the table until only the bone remained. She cracked it in half and sucked the marrow from one piece, then the other, before dropping them to the table.

"Is there anything else?" She twirled the knife between her fingers. Her gaze was fixed on the floor with calculated disinterest. Bruno knew she was waiting to see if anyone would challenge her weapon.

"No," he said, eying the knife, "that was all."

The knife disappeared with a flourish, and she strode down from the platform. Loddac hopped out of her way. From the workers in the corner she selected a bare-chested man who was well-muscled, leading him from the room by his belt. Loddac watched her with a look of lust or respect, but she only made Bruno feel uncomfortable. He disliked relying on her. "Lenir had better make his delivery," he announced to the platform.

Chapter 12

Dok proved correct; the freighter was ready the next day. Civilians were told, the word spread, and by mid-afternoon a line of dirty passengers snaked through Bruno's chamber. Their clothes were unfitting, hanging loosely over shriveled frames. Yellow dust caked their hair. But they were happy and hopeful, many for the first time in their life.

Bruno watched them with the solemness of the Praetari kings of old. He barely touched his food. Lenir had made no delivery, and with every passing moment Bruno's doubt grew. He began to second-guess his decisions. If he sent Kari that evening it would be another day before Lenir was replaced, and at least another more before Bruno could find out if the new foreman was malleable to his demands. If he'd killed

Lenir yesterday the whole process would be farther along, and he would be closer to having the parts he needed. But now he needed to wait.

He found himself staring at the bay doors that covered the wall to his left. He didn't know how sympathetic Akonai would be, but he suspected not very. The man was as cold and hard as steel. His demands were very specific. If Bruno could not deliver he would find someone who could, and whatever happened to the Lord of the Station would not be good.

"I ought to hire more guards," he mumbled, shifting his weight in the chair. A few of the passengers glanced up, but quickly looked away. Good guards were difficult to find. Most Praetari were as scrawny as this lot, wasting away from the Empire's food rationing. Strength was rare, and men were sent into the mines as soon as they could swing a pick. Bruno was forced to select boys, training them from an early age. Children were more obedient, especially when taught to rely on the Station for food and safety. But they required years to grow and train, and time was a resource Bruno lacked.

He could send recruiters into the mines. Working for Bruno was less dangerous than waiting for a mineshaft to collapse. Or he could march to the factory with his full force and take the parts he needed, foreman be damned. He would have the full amount required then, instead of waiting for a few shipments at a time.

But he dismissed the thoughts as quickly as they surfaced. Bruno had chosen his emblem with care. The massive desert snakes didn't slither in the open sand, where they were vulnerable to larger predators. They dug holes and burrowed, waiting for their prey to wander by. Man did not care to disturb a snake's burrow so long as it remained there. But if the snake killed a child, or wandered into the city, it could no longer be tolerated.

Bribing peacekeepers and skimming electroid parts could be ignored, but direct threats to their factories and mines could not. Bruno would not give the Empire reason to seek him out.

Kari arrived before nightfall. Dok giggled and stared at the assassin, whose vest revealed the tops of her breasts. She sidled up next to the him and arched her back in a stretch, sticking her chest out. She liked to tease the witless engineer.

Bruno offered her food, but she shook her head. "Do I have the job?"

There was no point in delaying any longer. Bruno nodded. "Tonight, as soon as possible. It must look like an accident."

"He would be at home tonight."

"I would assume so."

She hesitated. "I had hoped to do it tomorrow. An accident at the factory would be easier to stage."

"Consider it a challenge, then."

"I don't care to be challenged. I care to be paid."

"And you will," Bruno said. Was she acting strange,

or was it his imagination? Money was always an afterthought to the job itself. "I'll pay you extra upon completion, if you are concerned."

"I will be paid up-front," she said. "This job is more dangerous. The man is watched by peacekeepers at all times."

The insistence in her voice alarmed Bruno. He'd never doubted her abilities, but just then he wondered if the job was too difficult.

But another day could not be wasted; the foreman must die that night.

He pulled the square accounting device from his pocket and typed Kari's account with his thumbs. He entered some more numbers, and the device clicked and hummed. "It's done."

Kari pulled her own device from her coat's inner pocket. She stared at it a few moments before looking back up. "That is only half."

"You will receive the other half upon completion." She was definitely nervous. Something was wrong. "Half up-front is more than fair. I do not understand why you would need the full amount now, unless you mean to cheat me."

Her face hardened and she waved a hand dismissively. "No, this is adequate. The Melisao will die tonight."

Just then Kotra jogged past the line of passengers and into the room. "Lord Bruno, a cart just arrived out back."

Bruno leaned forward. "From the factory?"

133

"It's got the markings."

He turned to Kari and said, "Wait here. I may not need you after all."

She looked uncomfortable again. *Probably wondering if I'll want my money returned.* But that wasn't a concern just then. He didn't even care that the guards at the gate had once again failed to notify him of a visitor. If the shipment had arrived his problems would quickly dwindle.

He even smiled. Things were falling into place.

Outside the passenger crates were still being unloaded from the workshop. The freighter stood ready, its engines idling. Behind it rolled a huge cart, backing toward them slowly. It moved on six wheels, each as tall as a man, grooved along the outside for better traction in the dirt. On the side of its rectangle chassis was a symbol, the identification of Lenir's factory.

Dok muttered to himself, "The parts, we *need* them, need to work..." He was frantic now that the shipment had finally arrived.

Bruno ignored him. The cart halted, rocking back and forth on its wheels. The engine hissed and then was quiet. A door opened on the front, and Lenir himself hopped down into the dirt. He took a nervous look around the courtyard.

Bruno greeted him warmly. "I was beginning to think you wouldn't come! You see? I told you it was possible, if you were properly motivated."

Lenir still looked afraid, as if he would be attacked.

"Put your guns away," Bruno said to the guards, "Lenir here is our business partner now." Rief and Kotra slung their weapons over their shoulders, but the foreman remained tense.

"The wheels are wrong," Dok said, "we need the shipment, we need the parts..."

Lenir eyed the engineer warily.

"Calm down Dok, you'll get the parts soon," Bruno said. He turned to the foreman. "Don't mind him. You brought everything?"

"We need the *parts*. Not enough parts, the wheels are wrong..."

"I brought them all," Lenir said. He gazed around the courtyard, stopping on Kotra and Rief, and the cluster of guards standing by the freighter. He looked up to the roof, where two more guards stood watching the men below.

If he wanted to stay scared, that was fine by Bruno. *Some men refuse to see what's right in front of them.*

"Bruno, I need the *parts*..."

"Yes Dok, the parts are here. They'll be in your workshop in a few minutes."

"No Bruno, the wheels..."

The engineer was annoying him. "What are you waiting for, foreman? Unload it before Dok has a seizure."

Lenir went around the cart to the front, climbing inside. It should have just been a button to open the cart's storage bay but he stayed there several moments. Dok was yelling louder now, and Bruno started to walk to the front to see what was taking so long.

Everything went to chaos.

The cart's rear door banged open; explosions rocked the courtyard. There was a stabbing pain in Bruno's his ear. Suddenly he couldn't see anything. He realized he was on the ground, and pushed himself back to his feet. The world was silent, muted. Men in white uniforms emerged from the cart two at a time. Guns were wrapped around their arms, and wherever they pointed green beams streaked across the courtyard. One peacekeeper aimed at Bruno, but another grabbed his arm and shook his head. They turned away and ran to the wall, taking cover behind the passenger crates.

Bruno's head rang, vaguely aware of his guards returning fire. The men on the roof forced the peacekeepers to take cover. There were four more guards behind the freighter, shooting from what safety they could find. He saw Rief, back by the door to the main chamber. It looked like he was screaming at Bruno, but he couldn't be sure.

He forced one leg to move, then another. Soon he was running, or as close to a run as he could manage. He stepped around a body with a smoking hole in his chest. Kotra. He didn't slow. The beams flew past his head, and his legs moved on their own.

His ears began to recover as he reached Rief at the door. He fired his weapons back into the courtyard while he yelled. "...get going! We need to get inside, Bruno!"

Bruno ran past him into the central chamber.

Everything inside was a mess. The passengers waiting to board the freighter were all still there. Some tried to flee, and others huddled against the wall with their hands over their ears. Children screamed and cried as more explosions rocked the building. A crowd of passengers piled around the front door, but it was shut and barred with steel bolts.

A woman holding an infant ran to Bruno but he shoved her to the floor in his rush to get to the platform. He bent to his chair and tapped a code into the keypad on the armrest. It took three tries with his hands shaking. Finally the armrest opened upward, revealing a gun within. It didn't snake around his arm like a peacekeeper's, and was outdated by two decades, but it would fire green beams the same as the rest. He hadn't used it in years, but it gave him some illusion of safety.

The chair was too exposed, so he fell behind the massive table of food. Dok was there, covering his ears and muttering to himself. "I told you, the wheels were wrong, not heavy enough for all the metal, *I told you*."

"Dok, I need you to go to your workshop."

"No parts, needed the parts..."

"Go to your workshop and turn them on, Dok."

The engineer rolled on the floor mumbling until

Bruno grabbed him by the shoulders and shook him. Dok stared up with innocent eyes. "Dok, listen to me. It's very important that you go to the workshop. Turn them on, all of them that are functional. Even the ones that aren't ready. Then open the big doors. Okay Dok?"

"Turn... them on..."

"Yes, all of them."

"All the rowbits."

"And then open the doors, Dok."

He nodded to Bruno and scrambled away, still nodding all the way into the workshop. Bruno watched him go, and then turned to the warehouse door. Akonai would be unhappy if they lost any, but he didn't have any choice. It sounded like the peacekeepers would be inside any moment.

A knife was suddenly at his neck, pushing against the fat. "Open the front door."

Bruno rolled his eyes without moving his head, anxious of the knife. Had it cut him, or was the blade just cold? "Kari."

"Open the door, Bruno." There was nothing lazy about her voice now; it held the fervency of fear. "Or I'll give you a red, wet smile."

A tickle moved down his neck. He was definitely bleeding. He stared into her eyes, and in a flash of insight realized why she wanted her payment up-front. "You knew they were coming. You knew the Station would be attacked."

138

She pushed the knife harder against his neck. "Open the damn door, Bruno!"

"I need to get to my chair."

She removed the knife. He pulled a rag from his pocket and dabbed at his neck; it came back red. Not a lot, but enough to make him moan. Until Kari planted a boot between his shoulders, pushing him forward.

He crawled the rest of the way to the chair, typing another code into the keypad. There were three echoing *clunk* sounds as the steel bars retracted. The front door swung open, pushing away some of the passengers around it. Several darted out, but no more than that, because suddenly there were screams from the hall. The doorway flashed green and then the cries went silent.

The rest ran from the door, scattering in all directions in the chamber. Bruno watched with horror as peacekeepers poured into the room. There was no cover so they spread out along the wall, searching for targets. The scrambling passengers confused them, and a few were shot, but most of the Melisao held their fire. One of the peacekeepers pointed a white gloved finger toward the platform.

"*Shit,*" Kari said. She searched around for another exit, but Bruno's guards were falling back into the chamber from the courtyard, shooting over their shoulders as they fled. Rief and Loddac reached the platform and jumped behind the table. Another explosion shook the Station. Glass from the ceiling fell in huge chunks, shattering on the table and the ground around them.

"Three more peacekeepers in the courtyard," said Loddac, breathing heavily.

"I counted four," said Rief. "There was one climbing to the roof."

Two more of Bruno's men reached the platform, taking cover and returning fire. The peacekeepers were at the courtyard entrance.

"Four, then. Plus the..." Loddac counted, "...twelve already in here. There's only five of us, six if you count her."

But Kari was already on her feet and darting away from them. She reached the wall behind the platform and leapt, grabbing a handhold seven feet off the ground. She pulled herself up in one smooth motion, placing her feet where her hands had been and leaping again. She climbed like that, half clawing half jumping, until she reached the open windows of the ceiling. There was already someone there, looking down into the room, and after a quick blur of motion he fell. Glass and half-eaten food flew in all directions as the peacekeeper smashed into the table. Blood oozed from his neck, which opened like a hinge.

"Fifteen peacekeepers, now," Loddac said. "Bruno, what do we do?"

Everyone was looking at him. Rief and Loddac, his two most loyal guards, and two others he didn't recognize. The peacekeepers from the courtyard were inside, moving along the wall to join the others by the front door. A thought came to him. If they could reach the courtyard, they could take Lenir's cart. If there weren't more peacekeepers on their way. He wasn't sure where they would go, but just then it seemed their only choice.

His mouth was opening to give the order when a noise stopped him. Unseen gears creaked and groaned after years of sleep. The peacekeepers ceased their fire. Every eye in the room, Melisao and Praetari, turned to watch the massive bay door open. It was slow, but everyone froze in place. Rust drifted to the floor as the door clinked upward, until it finally stopped. The wall was now a square of darkness, the contents of the warehouse hidden within.

Dok, you wonderful bastard.

For a long moment nothing happened. Everyone waited in silence. The few civilians near the door backed away slowly. Bruno held his breath.

Then they came, a row of ten metal soldiers walking into the light. The electroids were vaguely human-shaped, with thick arms and legs connected to a square torso. They were headless, the computers in their torso possessing all the sensory function. They marched in unison, weapons held in front of them, the sound of their steps echoing off the walls. Dok only had enough guns for half of them, but the rest held metal clubs. Another row emerged from the warehouse, and then a third.

141

When the first row was ten steps into the room they began shooting.

Everyone jolted back to motion. The passengers ran in all directions. One peacekeeper barked an order, and the others fell prone to return fire. They shot wildly then, no longer caring if they struck civilians.

The electroids fired back steadily and indiscriminately. The ones without guns loped forward, swinging at the civilians with their clubs. The screams of terror turned to screams of pain, and soon the floor was covered with dirty, bloodied bodies. The crunch of metal on flesh made Bruno's stomach lurch.

Dok scrambled back to the platform, falling behind the thick table leg. He looked pleased with himself, smiling widely at the group.

A few of the electroids fired at the platform, forcing Bruno back below the table. It jerked as beams struck it, and the smell of burning wood filled the air. "Dok, why are they shooting at us?"

"Programmed. Only desert dwellers... allies." His smile faded.

Bruno's head ached. The electroids were built for Akonai. Dok had programmed them to only recognize the desert-garbed men as allies; everyone else would be a target. Which was why they were killing everything in sight.

"Well get back there and turn them off, Dok."

"Can't turn off, not for ten minutes. Programmed

that way. Fail-safe. Akonai's instructions..."

Bruno stared, his mouth half open. They didn't have ten minutes. In ten minutes the electroids would wipe out the peacekeepers and everyone else in the Station. Including him.

For a moment he considered striking the man, but he cowered like a child, mumbling to himself. Instead Bruno looked over the table. Everywhere men were dead or dying. The only Melisao remaining were by the front door, but they were already beginning to retreat. Many of the civilians dropped to the ground to pretend to be dead, but the electroids saw them trembling and savaged them until they were still. There wasn't much time.

"I'm going to run to the courtyard with Rief and Dok," Bruno said. The engineer would be useless on the platform, but would be an extra target running beside Bruno. He mustered as much authority as he could into his voice. "The rest of you stay here and cover us. Then follow once we're through. Then we'll escape in the factory cart."

It wasn't the best plan, but to his relief they all nodded. He turned back to face the door. *I can reach it in ten seconds*, he thought. He would be exposed, but it was better than sitting at the platform waiting to die. He felt a surge of hope.

He took a deep breath, yelled something, and lumbered away from cover.

Gunfire sounded behind him as the others returned fire. He felt like a fool bouncing down the steps, certain he would be shot at any moment. But then Rief appeared by his side, and he heard Dok mumbling behind him. Rief took the lead as they reached the door. Only then did green beams begin to streak past them. They darted through the door into the open air.

The sky was a dark yellow, the stars obscured by hazy clouds. The courtyard was illuminated by the roof lights. Bodies scattered the ground like garbage. There was a burnt smell in the air, smokey and metallic. One entire wall was missing, to the left. The Station was crumbling.

He saw the cart, still in the same place as before. But his eyes slid past it, to the largest object in the courtyard. A new idea came to him, and in the fervor of the moment it seemed like the best idea he'd ever had.

His legs ached as he ran to the freighter. Its engines still idled. The cockpit was on the top, accessed by ladder, so Bruno reached up and climbed. Each rung seemed distant, every step requiring all of his effort. The others waited below him; there was no way for them to climb around.

Gun blasts sounded again, louder this time. He was dimly aware of movement at the chamber door. Loddac screamed something below him, crying out in pain. Dok was counting to himself while the others yelled at Bruno.

Finally he pulled himself over the top and into the cockpit. It was a single room, with three seats facing the instruments and window. Bruno climbed into the first seat, panting heavily. Rief came next, scrambling over his stomach to get inside. Then Dok's head appeared, counting each rung as he climbed.

He frowned down at him. Everything was Dok's fault. The cart full of peacekeepers, the electroids that attacked everyone and couldn't be disabled. All of it could have been avoided. He was at the cockpit door, looking around as if unsure how to get past Bruno. He began mumbling, and looked to him for an answer.

Bruno snarled and slammed the door closed.

Dok looked through the window, confused. He didn't understand.

I shouldn't have relied on someone so stupid, Bruno thought, pulling the harness over his shoulders. He had to loosen the straps as far as they allowed, and even then they just barely clicked together over his girth. The cockpit came to life with colored lights and a purring noise as he pressed a few buttons. Dok programmed the freighters to be as simple as possible, so untrained civilians could fly them. The route was already set, he need only turn off two safety systems and begin the auto launch sequence.

Others were at the door then, the two guards whose names Bruno didn't know. They shoved Dok back to the ground, and rapped on the window. He couldn't hear what they said, but their faces were afraid. The freighter shook, vibrating their image through the window. One fell as a green beam cut through him, but the other continued to yell at Bruno.

Pistons beneath the ship buzzed and pushed, tilting the freighter backwards. The guard held on for as long as he could, but eventually slid down the diagonal ship to the ground. The electroids poured from the chamber, spreading out and taking cover. Bruno watched as the humans in the courtyard were surrounded, flanked, and killed.

When the ship was vertical the pistons stopped with a bang. The back of the cockpit was now the floor, their seats facing the yellow sky. Blood rushed to Bruno's head. He glanced sideways at Rief. Was something wrong? Why had the ship not launched? The electroids stood very still, a silent, shiny audience.

He was unprepared for the explosion. The seat bounced roughly into his head. His teeth chattered, and he tasted blood. Smoke filled the side windows, obscuring their view. But the ship remained planted on the ground. Bruno didn't know what was happening but in that moment he thought he was going to die.

Then something pulled the smoke downward, like a massive vacuum. His side window cleared, and the electroids were much smaller than before. It took him a long time to realize they were in the air. The ship soared. Rief's eyes were closed, and he held onto his shoulder straps with both hands. Bruno allowed himself to smile.

He pressed his face to the window but was unable to see the Station below them. That was probably for the best. He'd spent his life building it up, collecting power and resources around him. He was not sure how much of it was left, but it couldn't have been much.

Bruno had never left Praetar; he was unaccustomed to

spaceflight. The trip was not bad, besides the rattling that wouldn't stop. Rief vomited all over himself, which put Bruno into a fit of laughter. Then his own stomach lurched, but thankfully held strong. For once he was glad to have skipped his meal.

The rattling relented, and soon their ride was smooth. Rief stared off to his right. Bruno leaned forward against his straps and realized they could see their system's star, Saria. On Praetar's surface it looked yellowish, but now he could see that was wrong. The star was red. He couldn't look in its direction very long. He turned away and blinked, the afterimage flickering across his vision. Rief continued to stare, completely transfixed.

There was a kick as a secondary engine came to life, and the freighter began to turn. The planet heaved in Bruno's window, and he could see the line where day changed to night. It was incredible how much there was to see up here.

The engine abruptly stopped. The straps at the end of Rief's harness now floated, weightless. They made it. *The blockade really must have been lifted.*

The ship would orbit to the opposite side of Praetar before roaring back to life to begin the transfer to Oasis. Bruno looked around the small space. The cockpit had no long-range facilities: no kitchen or toilet. The freighter was only made to ferry goods from the planet's surface to long-range ships in orbit, and flying to Oasis would push its limits. But it would get there, if Dok could be trusted.

From his pocket Bruno pulled the Melisao

accounting device. It still showed his balance in big, blocky numbers. He wondered how much things would cost on the space station.

He thought he could begin his business anew, if the Empire's grip wasn't too strong. He was certain there would be a market for illicit goods and services there. Deep down all men were the same, whether their eyes were blue or brown.

Rief pulled his gaze from the window now that the star was out of view.

Bruno looked back at his account balance, and began to doubt if it was enough. Bribes to forge credentials, sleeping quarters, other arrangements. It would be expensive. The longer he stared the smaller his balance seemed. He would need loyal men, and right now Rief was the only one he had, but if the costs were too high he may be better off starting alone.

He fingered the knife on his hip.

Rief's eyes were closed, his harness still strapped. He rested his head back against the seat, exposing his neck. It would be quick. Rief would do the same to him, if he had to.

Bruno's grip tightened on the blade. He wondered what weightless blood would look like.

Rief opened his eyes. "Ohh..."

Bruno followed his gaze.

On some nights, when the yellow haze cleared enough, stars were visible from Praetar's surface. There weren't many, a dozen or so, like pieces of broken glass in the sand. It was a rare enough spectacle that everyone would run outside the Station to look. They would watch for hours, until the haze returned to mar their view.

But up here, with Saria now hidden behind the planet, Bruno realized how blind they were. For the first time he could truly see.

There were thousands of stars, millions of them. Everywhere he turned they filled his vision. Most were barely more than pinpricks, but some had size and color, blue or yellow or orange. There was more light than dark. Even spots that seemed empty revealed flecks of light, if he stared long enough.

A sense of wonder and smallness came over him. He'd been so foolish, thinking only of the options in his own system. *This* was the true size of the universe. If each of those stars held planets... it was more than his mind could process. How had he ever been content with his tiny plot of dirt on Praetar? Out here Bruno could truly be a king.

Two stars caught his attention. They flickered in space, brighter than the rest. *That's not right*, he thought. Could stars move? These were definitely moving. And growing larger.

The stars exploded in space, twin bursts of light that threw shadows across the cockpit. His eyes burned from the brightness, and clamped shut. He thought he could see the light through his eyelids.

Though the light finally faded, it was several

heartbeats more before his eyes would open.

It was as if nothing happened: they were still orbiting above Praetar, and the explosions were gone. Were they mines, placed in orbit to explode on approaching ships? Why had they detonated before reaching them? Was it just a warning?

Rief looked at him, but he had no answers.

Bruno squinted out the window. Praetar was hardly discernable, just a black mass splayed out beneath them. The stars were still everywhere. He watched for a long time, but there was nothing else out there he could see.

"There," said Rief.

Bruno followed his finger. At first he saw nothing, but then a shape moved across the stars like a shadow. It would have been invisible, except for the light it blocked. What would cause that phenomenon? Bruno knew little of astronomy.

Two more flickering stars appeared from the shadow. Bruno realized they were racing toward the freighter.

"Do something!" he said.

"What am I supposed to do?" Rief asked.

"I don't know, *anything*."

He mashed buttons. The ship shook as the engines fired, pushing them off course. But it was slow, too slow, and the missiles adjusted to follow. Didn't the freighter have some means of defense? Why didn't it have weapons?

Dok, you stupid bastard.

The missiles struck the freighter, and then the thought was gone.

Tales of a Dying Star

About the Author

David Kristoph lives in Virginia with his wonderful wife and two not-quite German Shepherds. He's a fantastic reader, great videogamer, good chess player, average cyclist, and mediocre runner. He's also a member of the Planetary Society, a patron of StarTalk Radio, an amateur astronomer, and general space enthusiast.

Amazon reviews are critical to helping indie authors gain exposure. If you enjoyed this book (or even if you hated it!) please consider leaving an honest review on the book's Amazon page.

Tales of a Dying Star

Sneak Peek

of

Book II: The Ancillary

"Madam Custodian, there's a problem."

Beth continued drying her hair in the mirror, but shifted slightly until she could see the worker's reflection. Mark was his name, she recalled. He was standing in the doorway, looking uncomfortable.

"Javin's the Ancillary Custodian," she said, "not me." She tried to keep the annoyance from her voice.

Mark looked up but quickly returned his gaze to the floor. Only then did she realize she was mostly bare, with just a cloth towel wrapped around her waist. Two tours in the military had stripped her of all modesty. Javin understood that, back when it was just the two of them working on the Ancillary. He treated her the way he treated everything: like a machine, judged on its usefulness and functionality. And Beth functioned efficiently.

But these civilians that now infested the Ancillary were fraying her nerves. They were too civilian, caring about their appearance and clothes and everything else. Half the men oggled her when they thought she wasn't looking, and the other half doubted her command. She never suffered such behavior from other *steadfasts*, the class of Melisao who opted for multiple tours of military duty.

Even when the workers did respect her, they came to her with every little task, drowning her in the minutiae of the Ancillary. She was beginning to understand why Javin fled to the solar ring. If there were anyone competent to leave in charge she'd be tempted to do the same.

"It's Darren," Mark continued. "He had an accident in the third core."

"How bad? Is he dead?"

Her bluntness took him aback. "No, he's alive. But..." He trailed off, his face beginning to pale.

Beth sighed. "I'll be there as soon as I put some clothes on." Mark gave a sharp nod and left the room, eager to be gone.

Clean uniforms were across the living quarters, so instead she grabbed the pile of clothes she'd worn before bathing. White pants that fit tightly around her muscled legs, and a long shirt with sleeves that covered up to her wrists. Boots lined with metal, good for labor. And a plain brown vest and belt to keep everything in place, with her short combat knife hung from a loop. She didn't bother with her brown hair, which was uncombed and still dripped water down her back.

The female cleanliness room exited into the female living quarters. There'd been no need for gender-specific spaces until the new workers came. Now they were neatly divided by whichever body parts dangled where. That didn't bother her as much as now needing to walk twice as far just to empty her bladder. The old facilities were ancient, but at least they were close together. And it all seemed a waste, building new facilities for a station that would be fully dismantled in a few years.

Stubbornly, she took a shortcut through the male quarters. She made a point of doing so, emphasizing the uselessness of the segregation. A handful of men were awake, eating their breakfast at a table before their shift began. They nodded politely–her presence there was no longer surprising–but did not resume speaking until she was out of sight.

The male quarters emptied into a maintenance hallway. To her left was the communications room. In front of her were the personnel airlocks, used to reach the external comm arrays or the transfer laser when maintenance work was required. Beth shuddered, keenly aware of how thin the asteroid was at that spot. Just a few feet of rock separating her from the black, the empty vacuum of space. Even standing there in close proximity to the airlocks filled Beth with paralyzing fear.

She supposed that was one good thing about the arrival of the other workers: she need never put on a space suit and work outside the Ancillary. Javin had done all exterior work when it was just the two of them–he seemed to even enjoy it!–but with him gone *somebody* had to do it. At least as temporary Custodian Beth was in a position to make sure it wasn't her.

She reached the ring, the circular corridor at the center of the Ancillary that connected everything together. Every function of the station was built off the ring, like haphazard branches sticking out from a wreath. The third core was on the opposite end of the ring, so she turned left.

Another problem with the new facilities was that it warped her perspective. The old quarters she and Javin had shared were small, simple. A single space with four narrow beds and a desk with a computer, with an adjoining cleanliness room for bathing and excretion. Ceilings their heads barely cleared, and metal walls that had long since lost their paint. It was comforting, like a den an animal might crawl into for safety. It reminded her of the military asteroids in the outer part of the Sarian system.

But the new facilities were spacious and pristine, bright with new light. Which was a wonderful upgrade until one ventured into the rest of the station. Now the Ancillary's age, its thousands of years of use, was obvious, every flaw magnified. The ceiling of the ring was too low, its walls too narrow. The beacons nestled in the wall every few feet didn't shine brightly enough, and gave off a yellow, dirty light. She had to duck to pass through the blast doors that were spaced every fifty feet. Beth wasn't claustrophobic, but it felt like being deep within a cave that may collapse at any moment.

Except there were no caves out here. There was only the asteroid's millions of tons of iron and nickel, and the black beyond. That thought wasn't any more comforting.

She reached a corridor at the far end of the Ancillary. One hallway led to the dock where ships came and went, and the other led into core three. She chose the latter, typed a code into the security panel, and entered.

Core three of the Ancillary power station towered over Beth, tall and imposing, disappearing into the ceiling fifty feet above. Blue plasma swirled inside the clear cylinder, spinning up and down its length like a cyclone. Wires and tubes spread across the floor like tree roots, connecting to equipment within the walls, dispersing energy throughout the Ancillary.

Mark was crouched over Darren, another one of the maintenance workers. They were both new, arriving on the last shuttle two weeks prior. Darren was Beth's age, somewhere close to thirty years, she gauged. He lay on the floor with his back against the wall, his left hand cradled in his right.

He looked up as she approached, his face as white as his uniform. When he shifted she could see why: the tops of three fingers were sliced away in a clean line. The cuts were black, still giving off tendrils of smoke.

"What the stars happened here?"

Darren looked away, and instead Mark answered. "He was cleaning one of the transfer tubes when a failover bolt went through. It took his fingers."

"I can see that," Beth said. "Disabling the core isn't enough. You need to manually select which transfer tubes stay open, in case there's a failover event."

Darren nodded weakly. "I understand, I just–"

"No," she cut him off, "you don't understand. If you did you would have followed the documentation, and you wouldn't be missing your fingers." Her voice echoed loudly in the chamber. "You're lucky that's all you lost."

Darren stared off blankly as if he didn't hear.

She turned to Mark. "I understand Darren forgetting, but you should have been backing him up. Why didn't you check his work?"

This time Mark looked away, and Darren answered, weakly. "He was gone. In the cleanliness room."

Beth sighed. Javin somehow kept the workers on track, but under Beth's command they seemed to lose their wits. "Why did I need to come down here? Take Darren to medical, then come back and finish the job." Her instincts told her the wound needed to be cut and cleaned, and she *was* wearing her knife, but that was what the med room was for.

Mark stood. "Who will replace Darren? Two people are needed–"

"One person can do the job," she said. "I did it by myself for years before all of you arrived."

Mark frowned. "I was hoping to go down to the dock..."

Beth shook her head. "Get the work done or you'll envy Darren's fate."

She strode away before he had the chance to argue.

Idiots, all of them, she thought as she walked along the ring. The Ancillary was a power station, harnessing Saria's energy before sending it back to Melis. All of the star's wrath, captured and contained within the asteroid. The new workers didn't have an appreciation for the power, the danger of it. Darren's sloppiness could have caused significant damage to the core. Or worse: Darren could have been killed, forcing Beth to deal with the paperwork.

Javin would have laughed at her for being so cold and unflinching. But gore had never bothered Beth. A man's fingers burned away wasn't the most gruesome thing she'd seen, not even close.

When she was a child her father was proud of her uncaring behavior. Crushing bugs was all she did at first, but soon she was running through the woods on Melis, hunting hares and rodents.

Her younger brother was the opposite, born with all

the empathy Beth lacked. He would cry whenever she smashed an insect or brought home a kill, as if he truly mourned the animal's death. Her father only watched and smiled.

But that was a long time ago. Now her brother was a rookie on his first tour somewhere, and she was a veteran of two, stuck babysitting civilians on a hunk of iron far from any action. She wondered how her brother was doing, if he'd ever become hardened like Beth. Their father wanted to transfer him to the Exodus Fleet after his first tour, she knew. That should be an easy assignment. She hoped he would find a way to remain innocent, unchanged.

She missed him the most, more than her sisters. He and Beth were the youngest of the four children, and their older sisters were more mystery than blood. Beth barely remembered Sandrakari, the eldest who was sent off to the espionage seminary at age ten. She was nothing but a name.

Beth had more memories of Pavani, but she was one of the Shieldwardens now, always at the Emperor's side. Beth tried visiting her the last time she was on Melis but the closest she came was a few hundred feet. From that distance her sister was a blue-armored figure next to the Emperor, taught and alert like a coiled snake.

It was years since she'd seen her father, too. He was too distinguished for standard tour lengths, spending all of his time with the Exodus Fleet preparations. She wondered if he ever thought of Beth, or if he was as cold and uncaring as she.

"You're not uncaring," she knew Javin would say. "You just don't flinch away from the uncomfortable."

Whether it was true or not, the words soothed her. Javin was more of a father to her, anyways, after their years together on the Ancillary, though in truth he was old enough to be her father's father. He only completed the one mandatory tour when he was young, and had never composed a family. She pictured him bouncing a baby on his lap and laughed to herself. The old man was uncomfortable with anything that couldn't be programmed with code.

She passed a worker in the hallway carrying a box of electronics in her arms. She nearly bumped into Beth, mumbling an apology before hurrying along.

Beth smiled. Javin would have called all the workers sloppy and complained that the Empire was falling apart. He didn't mind if an electroid malfunctioned, because there was always a definitive cause, a problem that could be identified and fixed. But humans were vague, confusing. A human could be thoroughly trained, and given documentation for reference, and he would still forget to manually choose the failover sequence before sticking his hand in a transfer tube. It only frustrated Beth, but it *confounded* Javin.

The stress was getting to him, she knew. She heard it in his voice on the last flyby. He may have initially gone to the solar ring to avoid all the Ancillary workers, but now he stayed out there because their work was behind schedule. No matter the cause, he would suffer the blame if they were delayed. As if dismantling the ring, the structure he'd spent his entire life maintaining, wasn't painful enough.

She came to a crossway in the hall and stopped. The living quarters lay ahead. Her hair was still wet and uncombed, but that was just another excuse to put off her duties. With a sigh she turned left, down the hall that led to the command room.

The command room was a wide rectangle on the outside of the asteroid, with the edge of Saria just in view outside the long window. Endless terminals and screens along the walls displayed data: station alignment, battery charge, core temperature. The energy needs of the entire Melisao Empire flowed through this room.

The Ancillary functioned automatically, in normal circumstances. One massive photovoltaic receptor was fixed to the side of the asteroid facing the ring, where the panel groupings discharged their power as the Ancillary flew by. The power was collected in batteries, then transferred to the four plasma cores in the center of the asteroid. Then when the Ancillary aligned with Melis, every ten days, the power was fired from the external laser in one long burst. A relay station similar to the Ancillary was placed on Melis's moon Latea. It received the energy, and from there it could be sent to the shipyard or planet surface.

But the dismantling process meant power was harvested from the ring unevenly. The Ancillary was aged, and reacted poorly to the disproportionate power collection. Javin called it "moody". Three technicians sat in front of a variety of computer screens. They didn't appear to be doing anything more than stare at data, but Beth knew they were focused, ready to rearrange the battery and core load as needed. Theirs was the most critical job on the station.

A fourth person sat against the wall. Elo was the Custodian's assistant–*Javin's assistant*, she thought stubbornly–sent to the station when dismantling began. He monitored the rest of the workers and relayed all important information.

And with Javin gone, that information went to Beth.

"Madam Custodian!" Elo said, rising from his seat. He was short and pudgy like a child, though he was several decades older than Beth. His head was bald and fleshy. A portable computer nestled in the crook of his arm, and he rocked back and forth on his heels while he waited for acknowledgement. Beth saw a long list of information there, waiting to be explained to her. She tried not to groan.

"I'm not the Custodian," she said.

"You are until Javin returns," Elo said, "but that's what I wanted to tell you. We're nearing the third quadrant. Javin's ship is returning."

54589296R00092

Made in the USA
Charleston, SC
06 April 2016